A World of Soma

A World of Soma

A Utopic, BioPsychological* and
Happy Science Fiction Novel

Zvee Gilead

*)   Biopsychology is the application of the principles of Biology (and
in particular, Neurobiology) to the study of physiological, genetic and
developmental mechanisms of human Behavior

iUniverse, Inc.
Bloomington

A World of Soma
A Utopic, BioPsychological* and Happy Science Fiction Novel

iUniverse books may be ordered through booksellers or by contacting:

iUniverse
1663 Liberty Drive
Bloomington, IN 47403
www.iuniverse.com
1-800-Authors (1-800-288-4677)

ISBN: 978-1-4620-1976-2 (pbk)
ISBN: 978-1-4620-1978-6 (clth)
ISBN: 978-1-4620-1977-9 (ebk)

Printed in the United States of America

iUniverse rev. date: 06/27/2011

"If we could sniff or swallow something that would, for five or six hours each day, abolish our solitude as individuals, atone us with our fellows in a glowing exaltation of affection and make life in all its aspects seem not only worth living, but divinely beautiful and significant and if this heavenly, world-transfiguring drug were of such a kind that we could wake up next morning with *a clear head and an undamaged constitution*—then, it seems to me, all our problems (and not merely the one small problem of discovering a novel pleasure) would be wholly solved and earth would become paradise."

> *Aldous Huxley, 1931. A quote taken from "required: a new pleasure" which appeared in a collection of Huxley's essays entitled "Music at Night."*

"Therefore the redeemed of the LORD shall return, and come with singing unto Zion; and **everlasting joy shall be upon their head**: they shall obtain gladness and joy; and sorrow and mourning shall flee away.

> *Isaiah 51:11 (King James Bible)*

"Don't worry, be happy"

> **Guru Meher Baba (1894-1969)**

Prologue

The Declaration of Independence of the United States lucidly expressed ideas on humanity's striving for happiness: "We hold these truths to be self-evident, that all men are created equal, that they are endowed by their Creator with certain unalienable Rights, that among these are Life, Liberty and **the pursuit of Happiness.**"

Success in the pursuit of happiness does not come easy. Being sentient human beings means, almost by definition, being imperfect, "scratched" and scarred . . . Many of us *do succeed* in the pursuit of happiness in spite of our imperfection. But, there are multitudes of men, women and children who cannot pursue happiness even if they tried – they suffer from depression or various mental disorders. For them, the *science-fictional* part of my book describes a marvelous drug invented by four scientists **that eliminated depression, mental disorders and drug addictions and opened an epoch of bliss and peace for all humanity.**

The book also contains a *non-fictional* part which brings basic information on the structure of the human brain and its functioning, about the causes of depression and mental disorders and describes how new drugs are developed. These non-fictional parts resemble a collection of "Reader's Digest" articles: They bring information on a variety of psychological and biological subjects in a concise way. To compile all this packaged data in my special "Reader's Digest" issue, I gathered information from many sources and set them in the book in a way which could save the reader much time trying to find and assimilate a lot of scientific and psychological data.

Part of the scientific information that I brought is accurate, although somewhat simplified for the sake of clarity. Another part is fictional and invented, as befits a science-fiction novel. Some scientific descriptions in the book may bore readers whose studies did not include biology. Still, in my opinion, any intelligent person in our times could benefit by reading them.

All that you will read below happened in a Utopia[1]. However, I know that there may be some readers (only a small minority . . .) who may dislike the book and say: "We love utopias. But who wants to read about depression and mental disorders? Why should we read about other peoples' problems? We would rather read

---

[1] **"Utopia"** translated from Greek as "the good place", or "no place", is any society governed by an ideal socio-politico-legal system. It refers, in its accepted and most general form, to a hypothetical and fictional perfect society. The description "Utopic" frequently refers to good but impractical ideas that cannot be implemented socially, economically or politically. The term "Utopia" was coined by Thomas More in his book from 1516 which was written in Latin and was called "On the good republic which is present in the new island Utopia".

"happy" romantic books . . ." I want to tell these readers that "A world of SOMA" is also a cheerful, romantic book!

In the face of our materialistic, cynical and belligerent times, my book is somewhat out of place . . . It is a "sweetish", naive book. Everything about it spells "doing good unto others". Unfortunately, good things do not widely happen in our real harsh world.

"A world of SOMA" is a *fairy tale*, a *utopia* that uses materials taken from a sophisticated world that practices science, psychiatry and biotechnology rather than from a world of witches, fairies, gnomes and elves. I pride myself that it is like a sweet dream in which everything goes so well that you would like it to continue as much as possible and will carry it into your day, dwelling on it from time to time with a smile.

To those of you who consider fairy tales to be suitable only for children, I can say that "A World of SOMA" describes the history of a really fortunate and happy world that exists somewhere in a "parallel universe[2]" – a world that we can only watch across time and space with envy . . .

---

[2]   **Parallel universes**, also called "alternative universes", "parallel worlds", "alternative realities", and "alternative timelines" are a hypothetical set of multiple possible universes. The term was coined in 1895 by the American philosopher and psychologist William James. The idea of parallel universes plays a part in astronomy, religion, philosophy, psychology, fiction - and most notably, in science fiction and fantasy.

1

Year 2013

It was a lovely January day in Boston. The skies were gray and cast with clouds and soft snowflakes fluttered down covering the naked tree branches with a dazzling white coat. Professor John Novick, an Associate Professor *from the Department of Neurochemistry of Harvard University's School of Medicine* was going to start a new research project. Little did he know on that day that he was going to participate in a saga which will bring peace, serenity and happiness to all humanity!

He was a tall, slightly chubby individual with black hair, a large mustache, brown eyes and an energetic, keen appearance. On that morning he waited to meet two persons: a young post-doctoral fellow, Dr. Benjamin Fond, who just graduated from the department of Neuroscience of the University of Pennsylvania Medical School and a young Ph. D. candidate, Debra Cohen, from the program of neurochemistry in the Harvard Graduate School. He was glad to enlarge his presently small group. In the last five years he had four graduate students who already finished their thesis work, obtained their Ph. D. degrees and left for various post-doctoral positions in other universities, as is the rule for graduating Ph. D.s.

First he was going to meet Miss Debra Cohen. When Miss Cohen phoned several days ago to fix an interview, she told him that she had attended his "Introduction to Neurochemistry" course in the graduate school last term and after reading on his current research interests, she decided to try to join his laboratory. Professor Novick remembered her as a student who asked intelligent questions at the end of each lecture and received top grades in his course. He also was quite taken at the time by her good looks, thinking that here is an example of beauty and intelligence combined together.

At the appointed time, the lovely girl that he remembered entered his office. Up close he saw a girl with black curls, a face of symmetry and beauty, black soft eyes and a lovely figure. While shaking her hand, he hoped that her beauty would not distract him too much from his research. He asked her to sit, prepared coffee for both of them and the interview began. At his request, she handed him her Curriculum Vitae and list of grades in the undergraduate and graduate courses which she attended. He quickly read them and said: "Miss Cohen, like all the scientists in the department I would love to enlist as many bright graduate students like you that I can. Therefore, if at the end of the interview you will still want to join us, I will be happy to accept you to my group and will try to make your stay here enjoyable and profitable for both of us."

Miss Cohen said: "Thank you Professor Novick. Please, call me Debbie. I don't need to wait for the end of the interview: I am very glad for the opportunity to work under you." Professor Novick thought that the term "under" that Debbie used was not a very good one since it conjured up in his mind a scene that he immediately dismissed . . .

Professor Novick said: "OK then, it is settled. Welcome and good luck in your work! Debbie, please call me John. You, I and the rest of our team are going to work on a project that has both academic and applied science aspects: the development of a new anti-depressant drug based on the Beta Endorphin neurotransmitter. You will work on some very important aspects of its development and I am sure that you will be able write a very respectable Ph. D. thesis on your part of the work."

They left the office, entered the lab and John introduced Debbie to Mrs. Lucia Fernandez, a Pharmacist and his trusted colleague who had been working with him since the beginning. He told Debbie that she can start whenever she wanted and she answered that she would like to start immediately. John assigned her a laboratory bench, a desk and a computer. He also asked Lucia to show Debbie the lab and apologized for not doing it himself, because he is shortly scheduled to meet a new post-doctoral fellow who is also going to join their group. He shook her hand again and almost drowned in her black, lovely eyes. For a second he imagined that he saw in them some promise, but immediately drove the thought away as an absurd one.

Debbie settled in her desk, started a search in the Internet for scientific publications on Beta Endorphin and thought: "Great, I was accepted to John's lab to work on a subject that looks quite interesting. Here am I, a granddaughter of Jewish immigrants from Russia, in the famous Harvard's graduate school waiting to embark on a new scientific career! When I attended John's Neurochemistry course I fell in love with him and now I am close to the subject of my love. During his course we gossiped about him and one of the girls, a distant relative of his, said that he is divorced. I hope that now he is not in a relationship. During the interview I looked straight into his eyes and tried to "broadcast" that I am romantically interested in him. I hope that he got the message. I will continue to "woo" him, to broadcast that I am interested and hope that he will eventually receive my "transmission." True, I am ambitious and being attached to him may help me academically. But, much more than just fulfilling my ambition I want to love him and to wipe the sad lines that seem to cloud his brow."

John sat in his office waiting for his second "recruit" and summed up his meeting with Debbie. "Wow, what an impressive and beautiful girl. I already feel strongly attracted to her. Her Curriculum Vitae said that she is not married, but such a lovely girl is most certainly in a relationship. Even if she is not, I definitely cannot ask her to go out on a date with me. She is 13 years younger, which is an obstacle. But, much more than that, since I am her thesis supervisor it is against Harvard's unwritten law to ask a student out to a date . . ."

A few minutes later John heard a voice asking for him and Lucia's directions to his office. He rose from his desk, went to the lab and looked interestedly at the newcomer, receiving a similar inspection in return. They shook hands warmly and John invited Dr. Fond to his office. John saw a young man with brown hair and brown eyes, muscled and of medium height. He handled himself with easy assurance and his eyes had an impish look in them. John said: "Dr. Fond, I am very pleased to welcome you to the Neurochemistry department and to our small group."

Dr Fond said: "please Professor Novick, call me Ben. Thank you for accepting me."

John said: "I'll call you Ben only if you would call me 'John', in spite of the obvious awe in which you hold me because of my great age, 35 yrs and my wisdom." Ben looked askance at him and they both laughed. Then John said: "Ben, let us go to the lab and I will introduce you to the members of my little group." John introduced Ben to Debbie and to Lucia and then he went proudly around the Lab showing his domain to his two new recruits. He also showed Ben the office that he had re-modeled for him from a former spacious chemicals' storeroom and then invited him back to his office.

John said: "Ben, we have a lot to cover to-day. First, let us start with some administrative matters. I will introduce you to Jeanne Dougherty, the Department's executive secretary. She will take care of all the required arrangements for you such as the issue of a Harvard identity card, a parking permit and access for you and your wife to all of Harvard's medical services. You are entitled to 3 weeks of leave and the right to attend one scientific convention per year in the country or abroad with all expenses paid. We have a large departmental library with all the important pharmacological and neurochemical Journals. Lucia will fill you in on everything else that you need. Once every two weeks we have a departmental seminar where each member lectures on any subject of his or her choice – their own research or on some other interesting subject. In addition, you can spend your whole week listening to guest lecturers from all over the country and from abroad. All of them consider it an honor to be invited to lecture at Harvard.

Now I would like to discuss with you a subject that I particularly like: namely, myself . . . I am a native Bostonian, my parents still continue to reside in Boston and I have a married sister with 3 children that I adore. I, myself, do not have any kids—my ex-wife could not conceive in spite of several fertility treatments. A year ago our marriage ended, mostly through my own fault. I am a recluse by nature and feel ill at ease in company. I spent too much time in the lab and neglected my wife who often went out with friends and finally found someone more suitable than me.

I was a top student in high school, applied to Harvard College and was accepted. This was no mean feat, since a lot of excellent high school graduates apply to Harvard. For example, in the year that I applied,

Harvard had an overall admittance rate of 8.3% chosen from about 25,000 applicants. What most Colleges call "Majors," Harvard terms "fields of concentration." Since I was interested in brain research I enrolled in a "special concentration" called the "Mind/Brain/Behavior Interfaculty Initiative", a program in Neurosciences run jointly by the departments of Anthropology, Biochemical Sciences, Biology, Computer Science, History of Science, Linguistics, Philosophy and Psychology. My choice of this special concentration program plus my excellent grades helped me to get accepted later to Harvard's graduate school as a Ph. D. candidate.

The subject of my Ph. D. thesis which was performed under the supervision of Professor Jim Schwabe from our department, was "synthesis of new derivatives of Serotonin with enhanced neurotransmitter activity." My thesis received praise and also helped me to obtain a postdoctoral position in our own department. This was unusual since, generally, postdoctoral training is supposed to be carried out in a different university or institution than the one from which you graduated. After my post-doctoral work, again with professor Schwabe's help, I obtained an assistant professorship position which is the goal of many aspiring young scientists. Now I am an associate professor with tenure and with a respectable list of publications.

We have good financial support for our project. A year ago I wrote a grant proposal to the National institute of mental Health (NIMH), which is part of the National Institutes of Health (NIH), and received a grant of 300.000$.

Ben, it is obvious to me from reading your Curriculum Vitae and the papers that you and thesis supervisor published together that you have a very good grounding in both in Neurochemistry, Biochemistry and molecular Genetics. Therefore, you will be able to supply the exact kind of expertise that we need for our joint project. I learned from your curriculum vitae that you and your wife lived in Philadelphia prior to coming to Boston. I would like to ask you whether you need my help in anything. Did you find an apartment? As a native Bostonian I can help you with whatever you need.

Ben said "Thank you John. After you accepted me, my wife Moira and I came early to Boston and rented a 2-bedroom apartment on Massachusetts Avenue and Pleasant Street, so that we are settled in. My wife is a paintings' restorer and found a job in the Harvard Art Museum which, as you know, is close to our apartment. Now I am all ready to learn about our new project."

Ben said: "After I have built everything to a climax, it is time to describe it . . . You, Debbie, Lucia and I will work on the development of a new anti-depressant drug that is based on the Beta Endorphin pleasure-inducing neurotransmitter."

"Excellent" said Ben enthusiastically. "I will be happy to work on such a project. I had a close friend in Philadelphia who suffered from Major Depression and was hospitalized several times. He was enmeshed in depression as a fly trapped in a spider's web, in spite of the many anti-psychotic drugs that were prescribed for him. I had accompanied him during his agonies saying that, as a neurochemist, I am fairly certain that it is just a matter of short time before a new really efficient drug for Major Depression will be developed, but to no avail—He committed suicide in one of his leaves from the mental hospital. I am also interested in the subject of anti-depressants since I am a little depressive myself and take a Seroxat pill every day."

John gave a start and responded immediately lest Ben will construe his reaction as criticism: "Dear Ben, You have certainly come to the right place. I am slightly depressive myself. I also took Seroxat In the past and then switched to Cipramil, which works better for me. The psychiatrist who treats me says that according to his reckoning one quarter of the population in the US takes an SSRI[3] or SNRI[4] pill of one type or another and those who do not – should take one because of the anxiety, worries and economical pressures they face every day!" Both scientists then entered into an animated discussion concerning the pills that they take and their side effects and this quickly bonded them together as soul-mates – brothers in a fight against a common "enemy."

Ben said: "John, I understand the need for a new really good anti-depressant drug. However, I can foresee that Debbie and Lucia will ask you why we need to develop a new drug in addition to the current SSRI and SNRI drugs."

---

[3]   **SSRI**-Selective Serotonin Re-uptake Inhibitor

[4]   **SNRI**-Selective Noradrenalin Re-uptake inhibitor

John said: "You quite are right, Ben. I will tell them that SSRI and SNRI drugs work well in cases of mild to medium depressions or anxieties. But that much larger concentrations are required for Major depression, resulting in intolerable side-effects. I will also tell them that the mechanism of action of the SSRI and SNRI drugs in the brain is not a natural process and this is why, possibly, these drugs induce side-effects. SSRI and SNRI drugs are known to prevent the destruction of the pleasure-inducing Noradrenalin and Serotonin molecules that is caused by the process of their re-uptake into the neurons."

Then John said: "Listen, Ben, I am soon going to lecture in an "Introduction to Neurochemistry" course that I teach every term. If you agree, you can accompany me to the lecture. On the way I back I will introduce you to the various members of the department." John agreed and then John apologized, requesting five minutes to go over his lecture notes and they went together to the lecture hall.

John started his first lecture of the course and said: "Good day to all of you. I bid you welcome to the spring term and wish you all success and enjoyment in my course. We will have one mid-term exam after the spring recess and a second one at the end of the term. The exact dates of the exams will be given to you later, as we progress in the course. Before I start, I would like to introduce Dr. Ben Fond, who just joined my lab. I will ask him to give one or two lectures later on in the course." John rose in his seat, waved and sat back again. John continued: "Dr. Fond obtained his Ph. D.

degree from the Department of Neuroscience of the University of Pennsylvania medical School and elected to come to the best laboratory in Harvard's Department of Neurochemistry – namely mine . . . I would also like to mention that I still have two positions open for new graduate students, so hurry before they are taken." John's blatant bragging and self-advertising brought smiles to the faces of some of the students.

John continued: "And now to the real business at hand: Paul MacLean, a scientist in the National Institute for Mental Health, described in 1952 a model for the human brain which came to be known as "MacLean's evolutionary three-brain theory." This model is still popular among some neurochemists, but is not accepted by researchers of comparative biology and evolutionary brain anatomy. I will describe it since it will simplify my explanations and descriptions of the human brain and its operation.

MacLean proposed that the human brain is composed of three brains that evolved sequentially during the millennia: the *Reptilian Complex,* the *Limbic system* and the *Neocortex.*

1) The *Reptilian brain* or *Reptilian Complex* first appeared in evolution about 500 million years ago. It includes the Brain Stem (a thickening of the spinal chord) and the fan-shaped Cerebellum (Latin for "little brain"). The Reptilian Complex controls muscles, balance and autonomic functions (e.g. breathing and heartbeat) and never stops working.

2) The *Limbic System* or *Limbic brain* appeared in evolution about 150 million years ago. It is situated above the brain

11

stem and is shaped like a "T" letter with a curved, instead of a straight, horizontal bar. It contains 3 parts—the Amygdala, the Hypothalamus and the Hippocampus. The *Limbic System* is the source of emotions and instincts (e.g. feeding, fighting, fleeing and sexual behavior). It can be stimulated to produce these emotions by directing a mild electric current into it. The Limbic System houses the pleasure centers. MacLean observed that reactions in the limbic system are classified either as "disagreeable"—the avoidance of pain, or "agreeable" – the recurrence of pleasure. The Limbic System cannot function alone. It needs to interact with the *Neocortex* to process emotions.

3) The *Neocortex,* also known as the *Cerebral Cortex,* is present only in the brain of higher mammals and is responsible for higher-order thinking skills, reason, speech, judgment, abstract thinking, imagination and intelligence. It absorbs information and enabled the development of human culture throughout the ages. It contains two hemispheres and takes up most of the volume in the upper part of the human brain.

The brain can be likened to a huge switchboard that operates with neurotransmitter molecules and nerve cells called Neurons.

What are neurotransmitters and Neurons and what is their function?

Neurotransmitters are endogenous chemicals which transmit signals in the brain from one neuron to another or to a target cell in the body. Some Neurotransmitters are small organic molecules, while others are made of small proteins (peptides), in which case they are called *neuropeptides.* There are about 50-100 different types of neurotransmitters.

A *neuron* is a nerve cell that sends and receives electrical signals within the body and the brain. It may send electrical output signals to muscle neurons (called motor neurons) or to other neurons. A neuron may also receive electrical input signals from sensory cells (called sensory neurons) and from other neurons. The word "neuron" comes from the Greek meaning "a sinew, tendon, thong, string, or wire." An average brain contains about 100 billion *Neurons.*"

Professor Novick then paused, projected a slide on screen behind him and said: "The slide that you see is a schematic representation of the structure of a Neuron and the way it is connected to other neurons. In the inset of the picture you can see a terminal dendrite with neurotransmitter vesicles and a synapse. At the end of each lecture I will give you hand-out sheets containing copies of the slides that I am going to project. Be sure to file them among your notes since they will come in handy before your examinations. In addition, at the end of this lecture I will give you a list of recommended textbooks that you may want to study. Let me now describe the various components of a neuron which are shown on the slide:

Structure of a typical neuron and a synapse[5]

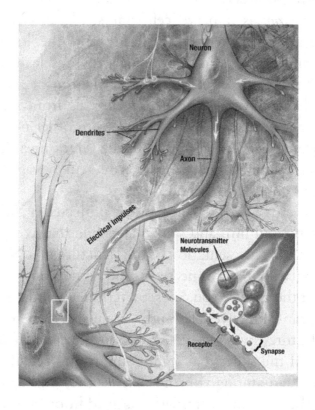

John pointed out to each item in the slide and said:

"Cell body – the cell body has an oval or polygonal shape and contains all the usual cell structures: the cell nucleus with its genetic material, mitochondria, cytoplasm, Golgi bodies, etc. Groups of neurons unite to create agglomerates that are called Ganglions.

Dendrites—dendrites are highly branched filaments emerging from the neurons' cell bodies. Their name

---

[5]   Courtesy of the National Institute of Aging

is derived from the Latin *"Dendros"*—*a tree,* because of their appearance. All communication between the neurons is performed by the dendrites. It uses electrical signals created by differential action potentials. These action potentials are produced by the in-and-out movement of ions of chloride, Calcium, Sodium and Potassium through ion channels that are present in the cell membrane of each neuron.

Axon – the axon is a long, slender fiber-like projection emerging from a neuron, which acts like an electrical wire that conducts electrical impulse from one neuron to the next one. In order to isolate the axons from their environment and to enable rapid transfer of electrical impulses, the axons are sheathed in an isolating layer called myelin, formed from *Schwann cells.* The myelin sheath contains gaps that occur at evenly-spaced intervals which are called *Nodes of Ranvier.* The axon with its Schwann cells resembles a string of "hot dogs." Axons agglomerate together into long strings which are the nerves.

Axon's terminal dendrites – axon's terminal dendrites are found at the far end of each axon. These dendrites are separated from the dendrites of the neighboring neurons by small gaps called *Synapses* across which impulses are sent. The name synapse comes from the Greek: Synaptein – "syn" ("together") and "haptein" ("to clasp").

As I have already said above, the brain is a huge switchboard and as such its neurons communicate with each other through the dendrites by a technic called "synaptic transmission" that occurs at the synaptic gaps.

As a result of the fact that there are 100 billion neurons in the brain and each neuron possesses about 1000 synaptic connections, there are more synapses in the human brain than there are stars in our galaxy. Despite this vast number of connections, synaptic transmission makes use of only two basic mechanisms: *electrical transmission* and *chemical transmission*. The latter mode is the one most commonly used.

Electrical transmission operates directly between neurons that are separated from each other by a very thin synaptic gap. Within this gap there are ion channels called *gap junction channels* that create bridges between neurons for the passage of the electrical impulses.

Chemical transmission occurs in the synaptic gap by the action of neurotransmitters. In the bigger image on the screen you can see a pre-synaptic neuron (at the top of the picture) that transmits a signal by chemical transmission from the axon terminal into the synapse and into the neuron at the bottom which is the receiving, post-synaptic neuron.

In the inset of the image you can see vesicles filled with neurotransmitters and one vesicle that had burst to release them. Also shown is a synapse containing released neurotransmitter molecules. The ejection of neurotransmitters from a vesicle occurs as a result of a transmitted signal.

In addition to the neurotransmitter vesicles, the axon terminals also possess myriads of *receptors* – small open pockets made of proteins that are shaped like "key-holes." These receptors accommodate their neurotransmitter "keys". When an electrical signal passes through the *transmitting axon*, neurotransmitters are released into the synaptic gap and diffuse to the dendrites of the next, *receiving* neuron. The diffusing neurotransmitters bind to the receptors and transform the *receiving neuron* into an *activated state* causing it to become a new *transmitting neuron* which passes the electrical signal to a new *receiving neuron*".

The lecture went on and when it ended, John led Ben back to their department and introduced him to its various scientists who wished him good luck and success in his research. When they came back to the lab, John glanced at his watch and said: "Ben, it is noon-time already and if you are hungry, let's go to lunch. We will discuss our project more extensively, also with the girls, first thing on Monday morning." The scientists entered the lab, took Debbie and Lucia with them and John said: "Ben and Debbie, we frequently go for lunch to Jack's Deli on Longwood Avenue which is about five minutes' walk from the lab. They serve the best hot corned beef sandwiches north of New York City. Since I want to commemorate the start of our project, all expenses are on me."

Lunch proceeded amiably and John realized that his gaze was drawn from time to time to the lovely Debbie who laughed at all his jokes, even the feeble ones. He found himself strongly attracted to her and in spite of Harvard's unwritten taboo concerning dating between professors and their students, he decided to ask Lucia to find out, discreetly, whether Debbie has a boy friend . . .

On the way back from Jack's Deli John asked Ben: "Tell me Ben, do you ski?"

John said: "I do, but not very well. My parents and I vacationed once in the Pocono Mountains when I was about 16 years old, but since then I did not have a chance to ski. Moira, however, skies quite well".

John said: "In that case, John, let me try to remedy the situation. If you agree, I would take you and Moira tomorrow to a fine ski site which is only about 30 miles from Boston and Moira and I will instruct you in the noble art of skiing."

Ben said: "Great, I would love to, but first let me check with my other boss." He called Moira and she was delighted to ski and to meet her husband's boss.

On Saturday morning John met the Fonds at the entrance to their building. John was very impressed with Moira, a slim and beautiful red-head. After the introductions they drove to the ski area and John and Moira spent a hilarious time instructing Ben and watching him stumble and fall until he finally gained some small mastery of the sport.

In the afternoon they had lunch at the ski site's restaurant. During lunch, John, Ben and Moira chatted about various parts of their biographies and John and Ben on their past scientific work. In addition, John became knowledgeable on picture-restoration as a result of Moira's descriptions of various aspects of the art. By the end of the day they parted as the best of friends.

2

Year 2022

In spite of the different time zones in the Globe, billions of Tri-D Holovision sets were turned-on in countless apartments and houses, Kazakh Yurts, Mongolian Gers, African thatch-covered clay huts, Eskimo Igloos, astrodomes on the moon and in various other types of human habitats. The sets were tuned to the news channels which were going to broadcast live, courtesy of WBR-Tri-D, Boston, a special address by Professor John Novick, the world's savior. To watch this broadcast in real time, men, women and children gathered in front of their sets even though it was late at night or very early in the morning in some time zones. Within every Tri-D Holovision "cube", the WBR-TRI-D newscaster was seen speaking and his words were simultaneously translated into the various languages and dialects of all countries in the world.

The newscaster said: "WBR-Tri-D is thankful for the privilege of bringing to you a historical broadcast of great importance – an address by Professor John Novick, the famous co-inventor of the SOMA drug. During his address you will also see his three colleagues who accompanied him during the process of development of the SOMA and still continue to work with him at Harvard – his partner to the two Nobel prizes Professor Benjamin Fond, Dr. Debra Cohen and his pharmacist technician Mrs. Lucia Fernandez. As you know, Professor Novick and his colleagues refused until now, to make public appearances other than the one they made at the Nobel Prize Ceremony. They did not want to be recognized on every outing and approached by grateful citizens. However, in the wake of countless entreaties from around the world, including from UN's General Secretary, Ravi Meenakshi, Professor Novick agreed to address the world, choosing WBR-Tri-D in Boston as his venue.

Until professor Novick starts, we will show you slides containing the announcements of both the Swedish Nobel Prize committee for Medicine or Physiology and the Norwegian Nobel Peace Prize committee on the winners for year 2014. We will allow enough time for the various stations around the world to translate them."

The Royal Swedish Academy of Sciences
6 October 2014, Stockholm,

Press Release

The Royal Swedish Academy of Sciences has decided to award the Nobel Prize in Medicine or Physiology for 2014, jointly, to **John Novick** and to **Benjamin Fond** from the Department of Neurochemistry, Harvard University *School of Medicine* **for their invention of the happiness-inducing SOMA drug**

This drug cured mental disorders that affected many people in the past – and, most importantly, brought great happiness and serenity to all humanity.

For the first time in the history of prizes, all the members of the Academy, unanimously and enthusiastically, voted for the two winning candidates of this year. All members believed that there had never been a single invention in modern times that had such an impact on the welfare and health of humanity like the SOMA. Moreover, our committee had to argue with the Nobel Peace Prize committee on the sole right for awarding the Prize. Finally, a compromise has been reached whereby *both* committees will award the prizes. This illustrates how important is Professors Novick's and Fond's contribution to the world.

Den Norske Nobelcomite
Oslo, October 9, 2014

The Norwegian Nobel Peace Prize Committee has decided that
the Prize for 2014 is to be awarded to:
Professors **John Novick** and **Benjamin Fond** from *the
Department of Neurochemistry, Harvard University School of
Medicine*

*for their success in bringing Peace to the world with the
happiness-inducing SOMA drug that they have invented. This drug
has brought peace, freedom from depression and oppression and great
happiness to all people in the world. It successfully eliminated all
wars, terrorist activities and conflicts in the globe. The peace that we
are now enjoying may be justly called "Pax Somatica". By awarding
the prize to these scientists, the committee wishes to express the world's
gratitude for their great contribution to the future and the welfare of
Mankind.*

The newscaster continued:

"It is worth mentioning that never before had two
Nobel Prizes been awarded to the same person *in the same
year.* Since the establishment of the Prizes, four persons
had been awarded two Nobel Prizes: Mary Curie won
the prize for Physics for discovering radioactivity in 1903
and the Prize in Chemistry for the discovery of Radium in
1913; Linus Pauling won the Prize for Chemistry in 1954
for elucidating the nature of Chemical bonds and the
peace Prize in 1962 for his action against above-ground
Nuclear Bomb testing; John Bardeen won two prizes in

Physics: for the discovery of the Transistor in 1956 and for the development of the theory of Super-conductivity in 1972; Frederick Sanger received 2 Prizes in Chemistry: for elucidating the complete amino acid sequence of Insulin in 1958 and for developing techniques for nucleic acid sequencing in 1980.

Then the newscaster said: "our channel controller signals that Professor Novick's address is about to start, so here it is":

The Tri-D image of the newscaster faded and that of Professor Novick appeared:

"Dear Viewers, we are lucky to live in a blissful world that the children in the audience probably believe had always been happy. But, until the invention of the SOMA, our world was immersed in a mire of depression, sadness and wars. Whole populations in many countries were poor and in grave danger to their lives. Even in the more affluent and strong countries there were men, women and children who suffered from depression and mental disorders and almost never experienced happiness.

Before the invention of the SOMA, well-wishing and wise people from various fields tried to alleviate depression:

Men of religion tried to console and to instill hope in the depressed. Shamans and Faith-Healers tried to drive away depression by rituals, incantations and various medicinal herbs.

Spiritual and mystic organizations advocated that depressed people must redeem their sins from past incarnations and after suffering in their present one, will gain everlasting peace and Nirvana after their death.

Psychologists tried to elucidate the cause of unhappiness and depression and to find the means to overcome it. Sigmund Freud, for example, maintained that Man's prime drive is to strive for pleasure and that those who failed in this striving, react by developing depression. Another noted Psychologist, Alfred Adler, believed that humans crave power and control and that their depression is the result of their failure to achieve it. Another opinion was expressed by Viktor Frankl, a survivor of a German concentration camp. In his 1946 book "Man's search for meaning" he stated that Man's prime motivation is to find meaning and significance in his life. He claimed that many people are trapped in an existential vacuum – a lack of a sense of purpose and direction. Frankl suggested that every man should overcome this existential vacuum by finding meaning in his life and targets to achieve. As a result of the findings of these and other sages, psychological treatments were devised that can, partly, alleviate depression. However, these psychological treatments may take years to succeed and are expensive. In my opinion, psychotherapy mostly succeeds in cases where the patients underwent painful traumas during their birth, infancy, childhood or adulthood. For others, the benefit of "shrinking" may be only marginal.

In Genesis 6:5 of the King James Version, we find the following verse:

"And God saw that the wickedness of man was great in the earth and that every imagination of the thoughts of his heart was only evil continually."

This verse was echoed in age-old philosophical discussions on the root of all evil and the sad situation of the

Human Condition. Scientists now claim that "evil" derives from our primitive reptilian brain. In some extremely evil people such as dictators and sociopathic criminals, the strong and continuous output of this primitive brain is not prevented or sublimated by the control of their higher brain, the NeoCortex (which is responsible for higher-order thinking skills, reason, speech, judgment, abstract thinking, imagination and intelligence). Following the administration of our SOMA to all people in the world, we proved that the age-old claim that "the wickedness of man was great in the earth and that the thoughts of his heart was only evil continually" is not true at all: euphoric and serene people are not evil – they are generous and considerate unto others . . .

With regards to depression, its causes and the ways to alleviate it, I believed that only a pharmacological-biochemical approach can cure depression! I maintained that the Great Creator, or Nature and Evolution if you will, made us biologically and psychologically vulnerable. We are not armored like turtles or partly immune to cancer or diseases like sharks, or long-lived like the Galapagos tortoises. We have a developed brain, an opposing thumb which helps us to hold objects and the subtlest and most adept vocal organs of all species that allowed us to develop speech. *But, our minds are sensitive and vulnerable.* Our brain resembles a complex computer that may contain bugs due to problems encountered during pregnancy and birth, or it can be affected by neurological, genetic and developmental defects that may cause mental disorders and depression. Neurochemists in recent years have proved that *depression is caused by an imbalance (excess, or scarcity) of important biochemical compounds in the brain.* They believed, as I did, that almost every person can be cured of his/her depression or mental disorder if we will re-adjust his brain's biochemical equilibrium. We ought to remember that men (aside from their "souls" and emotions) are no more than complex biochemical structures made from the atoms of Menedle'ev's periodic table of elements . . . Therefore, my colleagues and I were quite sure that the recent breakthroughs in brain research, genetic engineering, neurochemistry and pharmacology ought to lead to the development better anti-depressant drugs than those that existed at the start of our research.

Luckily for Humanity, my colleagues and I succeeded in our quest. As you know, we developed an anti-depressant drug which was extremely efficient, much beyond our wildest dreams and expectations!

Professor Fond and I won two Nobel Prizes for the year 2014. In my Nobel Prize address in Stockholm I said that I consider myself to be no more than a competent scientist who got lucky . . . and since I am a science-fiction fan, I also said that perhaps some higher entities planted the idea of the SOMA research in my sub-consciousness. I carried this "idea" even further and said that perhaps these entities wanted to save Humanity at the twelfth hour before we will annihilate each other in an atomic war or by chemical and microbiological warfare . . . Indeed, watching documentary films from the past, I am amazed to see how depressing and frightening were world news before the SOMA. Now, in contrast, people are so considerate, peaceful and compassionate, helping those in need, and abandoning all their earlier paths of greed, corruption, oppression and wars.

Therefore, every day and night I give praise in humble gratitude to all possible addresses – God, sublime entities, angels, aliens, collective—or my own subconscious mind that, perhaps, helped me to conceive the idea of the SOMA.

Those who would like to know more about the course of development of our SOMA are invited to read the book that Professor Ben Fond, Dr. Debra Cohen and I wrote: 'The road to happiness – the invention of the SOMA'. It can also be found in the Internet at "www.SOMA.com." This site contains translations of the book to almost all the major languages."

Professor Novick stopped at this point, drank some water and said:

"**Depression,** what a tragic and terrible word it was. Depression was a state of mind that manifested itself by gloom, a feeling of "cramped" heart, agony, shortness of breath, a decrease in self esteem, helplessness, hopelessness, guilt feelings, low concentration ability, suicidal tendencies, sleep disterbances, eating disturbances, reclusiveness, lack of motivation, sluggishness and lack of energy – quite a handful of troubles!!! All of these symptoms caused a serious reduction in the daily functioning of depressed people. Depression was also accompanied by anxiety, with all its physical manifestations: accelerated heart-beat, breathlessness, chest discomfort, dry mouth, fears of impending doom, or hypochondriac fears of incurring disease.

Depression occured in varying intensities: from passing feelings of dejection up to extreme cases of depression (Major Depression) which caused patients to remain hopelessly all the time in bed.

There were four main causes to the evolvement of depression:

1) Tragic and miserable life history, sexual abuse, incest and extreme environmental hardships.

2) Imitation of a depressed and worrying parent who broadcasted helplessness.

3) Genetically-directed individual brain biochemistry. In this case, depression was caused mainly by a disequilibrium of pleasure-inducing neurotransmitters of Serotonin, noradrenalin and Endorphin in the brain.

4) "epigenetic stamping" – *non-genetic* transmission of traits from the mother to the embryo. Some scientists believe that fetuses may be stamped in the womb with their mothers' depressions because of their strong (telepathic?) link to their mothers or through the effects of hormones and neurotransmitters passed to them from the mothers. How this transmission operates, if it indeed exists, remains still unknown even to-day and therefore many behavioral scientists scoff at it.

In 2013, when my colleagues and I started our research, a report of the World Health Organization stated that one sixth of all men and women in the western countries suffer from depression or mental problems of varying degrees. It also was predicted that the prevalence of depression will double itself within the next 20 years. The prevalence of depression was even higher among the elderly, compared to younger people. Many of the elderly suffered from loneliness, the death of their mates, poverty, chronic pains, lack of tasks to perform in the family and society, poor mobility and the wear and tear of their bodies and their functions. The awareness that their life was quickly drawing to its end worsened their condition. Biochemically, they suffered from a growing deficiency in the production of Serotonin, Dopamine and Noradrenalin molecules in the brain.

Before the SOMA, major depression was treated by electroconvulsive shock or with drugs that afforded only small relief. As is the rule with many drugs, they had serious side-effects. Milder forms of depression were mostly treated with antidepressant drugs of a group that was called "selective serotonin and/or Noradrenalin reuptake inhibitors (**SSRI/SNRI**). These drugs were used to treat not only depression, but also anxiety and personality disorders. **SSRI/SNRI** drugs exerted their anti-depressant effect by preserving the existing serotonin or Noradrenalin molecules in the brain by preventing their re-uptake back into the neurons and their subsequent destruction. Among these drugs were Prozac, Seroxat, Cipramil and many others. There were also other types of anti-depressant drugs in addition to **SSRI/SNRI**, that belonged to two other groups called tricyclics and MAOIs, but they are not used as much as **SSRI/SNRI** drugs.

I have to say that as a result of the development of the SOMA, many very big drug companies lost their revenues from anti-depressant drugs. However, the managements of these companies did not hold us any grudge since they became, like everybody else in the world, serene, satisfied and happy. They continue to invest money and efforts to produce good medications for the many other "physical" diseases of humanity.

Before the discovery of the SOMA, in a desperate wish to seek pleasure and to escape from their often miserable or harsh reality, many person, including adolescents, used dangerous "street drugs" that were sold by criminals. These drugs were illegal in most countries because they were strongly Psychogenic, i.e., they irreversibly damaged the brain and its functions. They also caused passing or permanent changes in consciousness, perception of reality, behavior and mood and were habit-forming. Those addicted to them required increasingly larger doses to achieve a pleasurable effect and became criminals who turned to prostitution, stealing and robbery in order get their "fix". They became the dregs of society and their bodies and brains deteriorated quickly until their early demise. This group of street drugs included ignominious and dangerous chemicals such as Alcohol, Crack, Cocaine, Ecstasy, Crystal-Meth, Opium, Speed, Hash and many others.

You may wonder why I chose the name "SOMA" for our drug. Well, as a young man I read a book called *"Brave New World"* that impressed me very much. The book was published in 1932 by Aldous Huxley, a British philosopher and biologist who was considered to be one of the creators of the new academic thinking of his time. The title of the book was taken from Miranda's soliloquy in 'The Tempest' by Shakespeare. In act 5, scene 1, Miranda says:

"O wonder!

How many goodly creatures are there here!

How beauteous mankind is!

O brave new world!

That has such people in't!"

The *"brave new world"* described by Huxley was a mythical happy world – a Utopia—located in London of the 26th century. Huxley "invented" biological disciplines that did not exist in his time such as genetic engineering, artificial insemination and organ culture. 'Brave New World's' citizens grew in bottles containing fertilized eggs. Huxley's *Brave New World* was free from worries, depression, wars and poverty and all its citizens were endlessly happy. All this was achieved by daily consumption of a pill called "SOMA" which had been developed by the *Brave New World's* scientists.

But Huxley, contrary to some of the optimistic utopian novelists of his time, sarcastically turned everything upside down and emphasized all the problems of his Utopia: stagnation, cultural atrophy and lack of any free thinking.

Huxley's name of "SOMA" was taken from Sanskrit, a historical Indo-Aryan language which was one of the liturgical languages of Hinduism and Buddhism. The Indo-Aryan "SOMA" was a ritualistic drink whose composition and source are unknown today. The ancient Vedic scriptures abound with hymns dedicated to this drink and both the indo-Persian and Vedic cultures attributed to it intoxicating and happiness-inducing properties. When we found out that the antidepressant drug that we developed was so efficient in inducing happiness, I decided to call it "SOMA".

After a few months of intensive work" ... thus continued the professor in his address but, concomitantly, in another part of his brain passed various vivid recollections from the various events of his SOMA research. The ability to think simultaneously in two different tracks was only one of the many blessings of the SOMA drug that he and everyone else of the world's inhabitants had taken daily . . .

3

Year 2013

On the Monday morning following the enlistment of Ben and Debbie, all the scientists sat in John's office and waited for his exposition of their future common research project.

John said: "At the outset, let me say that I was drawn into the study and research of anti-depressant drugs because of personal reasons: my mother, my sister and I suffer from mild depression while my father, a Vietnam war veteran, came back from war with a serious case of Post Traumatic Stress Disorder. To alleviate my own symptoms of depression, I take an SSRI drug called Cipramil which works quite well for me. However, it does have some side-effects, among which is a tendency for food craving and this is why I am slightly plump. On the plus side, It has some benefit – it is prescribed by sexologists to combat pre-mature ejaculation."

During his last words, John regretted the disclosure of his own depression but calmed down when he saw an expression of sympathy on Debbie's face (Lucia and Ben were already familiar with his plight).

Debbie thought: " 'Oy vey', as my grandparents used to say in Yiddish, I was right! John indeed looks slightly sad and worried despite his attempts at humor. In addition, he probably still smarts from his divorce. I wish I could erase the lines of depression from his brow"!

John said: "Debbie, you can take notes during my description of our project, since they will be of use to you when you start to write the "introduction" chapter to your thesis.

Currently, most biological theories on the causes of Major Depression focus on the role of the monoamine neurotransmitters of *Dopamine*, *Noradrenalin* and *Serotonin*. These neurotransmitters are molecules that contain one amino group that is connected to an organic aromatic carbon ring by a two-carbon chain. Depression, according to the currently favored "monoamine hypothesis", postulates that a deficiency of *Dopamine*, *Noradrenalin* and *Serotonin* neurotransmitters in the brain leads to depression. Thus, *Dopamine* is linked to attention, motivation and reward, as well as to interest in life. However, *Dopamine* can also be harmful. *Too much Dopamine* in the brain causes mental frailty, unexplained anxieties, deep depression, schizophrenia and aggressive behavior. *Noradrenalin* is related to alertness and energy, anxiety, attention and interest in life. However, *too much Noradrenalin* leads to fast emotional responses such as anger, quick heartbeat and a shift of oxygen and nutrients to muscles only and not to internal organs. *Serotonin,* however, is the best of all the above-mentioned neurotransmitters: an increase in its concentration in the brain leads to a mood of serenity and euphoria.

As you know by now, we are going to work on *Beta Endorphin,* which from now on I will simply call "Endorphin". This neurotransmitter, which is responsible for the "Runners' High" that appears after a strenuous exercise, is an excellent candidate for an anti-depressant drug since it does not cause any adverse effects. Besides, my reason for choosing it is that—and this is something that as yet is unknown to other neurochemists – *it strongly controls the synthesis of Dopamine, Noradrenalin and Serotonin!* During the last year I have made a ground-breaking discovery of which I am very proud. I have already written a paper on this discovery which is due to appear in the June issue of the prestigious "Journal of Neurochemistry." I hypothesized that Endorphin is the key controller of synthetic inter-relationships between the three neurotransmitters that I mentioned. I tested my hypothesis in rats: one group of rats received Rat Endorphin, which I bought commercially, while the other group received a sterile salt solution as control. I infused the two solutions into the Nucleus Acumbens pleasure centers of the rats' brains using very thin tubes. Thirty minutes after the infusion of these solutions, I removed samples of fluids from the brains by suction, and tested their concentrations of Dopamine, Noradrenalin and Serotonin. This infusion experiment may seem cruel to you, but the animals did not suffer since the brain lacks pain-sensing neurons and possesses enough fluid that bathes all parts of the brain. The results obtained were very clear. They led me to formulate what I call the "*Endorphin to Serotonin pathway.*" This pathway is summarized in a scheme which is taken from the paper." John handed the scientists a page with a scheme:

The Endorphin – Serotonin pathway

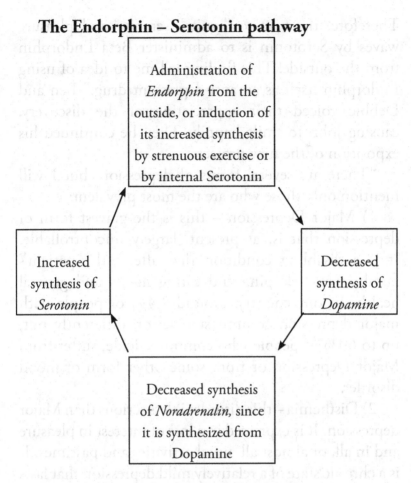

John said: "As you can see, high levels of Endorphin in the brain, administered from the outside, decrease the synthesis of Dopamine. A Dopamine's decrease, causes a parallel reduction in the synthesis of Noradrenalin and most importantly—this decrease in Noradrenalin's synthesis, induces an increase in the levels of the pleasure—and serenity-causing Serotonin! The resulting increase in the level of serotonin induces an increased synthesis of Endorphin and so on, in a circular fashion!

Therefore, the way to "ignite" serenity and pleasure waves by Serotonin is to administer Beta Endorphin from the outside! This finding led me to idea of using Endorphin itself as an anti-depressant drug!" Ben and Debbie voiced their appreciation of the discovery, causing John to smile happily. Then he continued his exposition of the new project:

"There are several forms of depression, but I will mention only those who are the most prevalent:

1) Major Depression – this is the gravest form of depression that is, at present, largely uncontrollable. It is a disabling condition that affects the patient's family, work, sleeping and eating habits and general health. In our country, around 3.4% of people with major depression commit suicide; or, differently put, up to 60% of people who commit suicide, suffer from Major Depression or from some other form of mood disorder.

2) Disthemia – this disorder is less serious than Major depression. It is expressed in a loss of interest in pleasure and in all, or almost all, usual activities and pastimes. It is a chronic state of a relatively mild depression that lasts for years. It affects about 3 percent of the population at any given time and is therefore, a very common form of depression. Disthemia is treated with a combination of psychotherapy and SSRI/SNRI drugs.

3) Postpartum depression (PPD), also termed postnatal depression, is a form of depression which affects from 15% to 35% of women in the first few months after giving birth. It piles on top of their lack of sleep during the first months after giving birth

until the babies start to sleep long hours at night. Its symptoms include sadness, fatigue, appetite changes, crying episodes, anxiety and irritability. Current studies show that it is mostly caused by the significant hormone changes that occur during pregnancy and take time to subside. Women are now more aware of this form of depression where, previously, they could not understand what hit them.

4) Bipolar disorder or manic–depressive disorder—this is a very serious disorder which is defined by the occurrence of episodes of abnormally elevated energy levels and cognition that are followed by depressive episodes. The elevated moods are clinically referred to as mania or, when milder, hypomania. Cyclical episodes of mania and depression are usually separated by periods of "normal" mood; but, in some individuals, depression and mania may alternate without a normal period in between.

The term "Endorphin" is an abbreviation of "Endogenous Morphine." Beta Endorphin is a very small protein – a peptide—which contains 31 amino acids. It is known to the general public as the material produced in the brain following strenuous activity such as jogging or extensive exercise.

How was Endorphin discovered? A group of biochemists studied the causes of opium addiction in 1960 and discovered a receptor for it in brain tissue. Since it seemed irrational from an evolutionary point of view to have a receptor for opium which is a plant material, the scientists searched for brain molecules that can bind to the opium receptor and thus discovered

Endorphin. The concentration of Endorphin is significantly increased in the brain in times of tension, sharp pain, during orgasm in men and women and during strenuous exercise. Chocolate and Chili peppers also induce increased production of Endorphin. This is why people turn to chocolate in times of tension and distress. Chili peppers are also used for the treatment of chronic pain and are sexual arousers. In addition, it was shown that massage, acupuncture, meditation and sun-tanning also induce increased Endorphin production. Even hearty laughter induces it and this phenomenon is utilized in "laughter workshops" that are now gaining a lot of popularity in many countries. The participants of these workshops laugh "artificially" at first until, gradually, everybody is "infected" with real laughter.

Ben, you will be responsible, together with Debbie, for the production of Endorphin in bacteria by Genetic Engineering, and for its purification. When we have enough pure Endorphin, we will administer it to people with depression and see if it will induce pleasure. It is quite possible that we may fail. But if it will work, we will gain fame and recognition and, more importantly, help countless sufferers. All the technologies and methods required for our project are already available and we just need hard work and a "favorable response" from the brain's physiology to succeed . . .

Ben, I want you to realize before we start that if we fail, I personally will not be injured since I already have tenure and Debbie on her part, will still have an interesting training time and a fine thesis. In case of failure, we will publish a paper describing the synthesis of Endorphin and note that it failed as a potential anti-depressant drug. However, it will not be a very important contribution and you will lose precious time in building a career for yourself. If you want, I can offer you a less risky research project".

Ben said: "John, even if we fail, I think that the goal that you set before us is worth any risk. Besides, doing post-doctoral work in the celebrated Harvard University will still help my career, even in case of a failure."

"Very well then" said John. "Dear colleagues, please forgive me for the banal clichés that I am about to say. However, they represent my Raison d'Etre[6]: I think that what I am about to say holds for most people working in the fields of Biology and Life Sciences: we do not earn as much as those working in High-Tech. But, on the other hand, our quests are sublime and exalted – working for the prolongation of life, improving health and alleviating suffering." Seeing that his listeners nodded their heads in agreement, John continued: "In fact, we should actually pay for the privilege of doing research, rather than getting paid . . . We spend our life occupied in a Hobby that we like, waking every morning in the hope that the next experiment that we will perform will be a crucial one that will extend the boundary of the unknown one step further and will contribute to the health of Humanity. It is true that our road is not always paved with roses: our work may not always succeed, causing us to fail in obtaining research

---

[6]   **Raison d'Etre** - French for "reason for being".

grants and in advancing academically. Even the general public is familiar with the phrase "publish or perish."

But, enough of that. Let me describe to you some scientific facts relevant to our project. You may be already familiar with most of them but I like to hear myself lecture, being quite good at it. In fact, I have been consistently voted as "the most interesting lecturer" in the Undergraduate courses that I taught. In addition, what I am about to say is intended for Debbie's "introduction" chapter of her thesis:

When a person suffers acute pain, pain waves travel from the damaged organ along his nerves up his spinal cord and to the brain. The brain, in an immediate reaction, secretes Endorphin that relieves the pain mostly in the brainstem. However, Endorphin, aside from alleviating pain for a while, also acts on specific neurons in the pleasure centers of the brain and induces serenity, self confidence and calmness, thus balancing pain. We know now that, according to my Endorphin to Serotonin pathway finding, it does that by inducing an increased synthesis of Serotonin which acts on the pleasure centers of the brain.

The pleasure centers in the brain were first discovered in the 1950s by James Olds and Peter Milner. These scientists inserted electrodes into various areas of the limbic system of rat brains that received an electrical current when they entered an electrified corner in their cages. The scientists were sure that the rats will quickly learn to avoid the electrified corner after the first few shocks. Instead, they were surprised to see that when the rats were driven away from the electrified corner by the experimenters, they ran quickly back to it, indicating that they enjoyed these electrical shocks. In later experiments the rats were taught to press an electricity-inducing lever that directed electrical pulses into their brains. The outcome was that the rats pressed the lever repeatedly as much as seven-hundred times per hour. They preferred pleasure over eating and drinking, with the result that they stimulated themselves to death.

And from rats to men: between 1950 to 1952 – that is before the discovery of the pleasure centers in the brain—Dr. Robert Heath, a psychiatrist from the Department of Psychiatry and Neurology at Tulane University, New Orleans, already performed electrical stimulation experiments in his mental hospital. He tested patients who suffered from schizophrenia, epilepsy and "phantom" pain by inserting electrodes into various parts of their brains and stimulated them electrically. About half of the patients reported a strong feeling of pleasure upon stimulation and freedom from attacks and pain. However, several months later, the experiments were terminated by the order of the mental hospital's management which justly believed that Heath's surgical procedure for the insertion of the electrodes was dangerous and can lead to infection and death. Interestingly, there is at present a more focused, advanced and successful return to Heath's electrical stimulation experiments in Parkinson patients. These patients are successfully treated with a technic called "deep brain stimulation" that uses electronic "pacemakers" implanted in their brains.

I want now to describe the steps that we will follow in our study. For that, I prepared a flowchart with a description of the steps of our future research and the division of the work between us." John handed each scientist a flowchart and said: "Note that at the start Lucia will not participate in the our study. She will join you in later stages since she still has to finish work a project that she and I started some time ago. As for me, I have to prepare lectures for a new undergraduate course that I am going to teach next term so that I will join you only after you will supply me with enough pure Endorphin for mouse and human experimentation. However, our whole program will be cut short if, God forbid, we will fail in any one of steps 6 to11.

Flowchart of the Endorphin project:

> **1. Isolation and multiplication of the Endorphin DNA gene**
> "Contractors": Ben and Debbie

↓

> **2. "Cloning" of the Endorphin gene into a DNA vector**
> "Contractors": Ben and Debbie

↓

> **3. 'infection" of E. Coli bacteria with the cloned Endorphin's DNA vector**
> "Contractors": Ben and Debbie

↓

> **4. Selection of the best endorphin-producing colony for future cultivation** "Contractors": Ben and Debbie

↓

> **5. Harvest of Endorphin from bacterial cultures and its purification**
> "Contractors": Ben and Debbie

↓

> **6. "Camouflage" of the Endorphin** "Contractor": John

↓

> **7. Testing the activity of the "camouflaged" Endorphin in mice**
> "Contractors": John and team

8. Testing addiction to Endorphin in mice
"Contractors": John and team

9. Preclinical safety testing of Endorphin in animals John and a pre-clinical research contractor

10. Testing of the efficiency of Endorphin in human volunteers
"Contractors": John and team

11. Testing addiction to Endorphin in humans "Contractors": John and team

12. **Preliminary clinical trials in patients**
John and team and various staffs of psychiatric institutions

13. **The signing of a partnership agreement with a major drug company**
Harvard's Technology development office

14. **Performance of extensive clinical trials with Endorphin in many medical centers for the certification of the SOMA by FDA**
Contract clinical research organization

John said: "I believe that the flowchart is quite clear, but I will still explain its essentials: we will produce Endorphin and "truncated" Endorphin molecules by genetic engineering in bacteria and will purify large amounts of them. "Truncated" Endorphin is an Endorphin from which we will cut 4 amino acids from one of its ends. It will act as a negative control in our animal and human experiments. Then we will "camouflage" both endorphins (whole and "truncated") so that they will be able to cross the Brain Body Barrier. I will explain this camouflaging thing to you later. Next, we will test whether Endorphin will have an anti depressant activity in mice. If it works well in mice, we will test it in depressed humans. Endorphin is an endogenous Opium–like (opioid[7]) drug. Therefore, if it will work on humans, we will have to test whether it will cause addiction both in mice and in humans, just as many opioid drugs do on prolonged use. If Endorphin is not addictive in humans, we will send it to a company that will perform for us pre-clinical safety testing in animals. Finally, we will hire the services of another company called Clinical Research Company (CRO) that will perform human safety and efficacy testing in order to obtain certification from FDA.

---

[7]   **Opioid (Opium-like) drugs** - these drugs belong to several classes: *Natural opioids (also termed opiates)* such as morphine and codeine which are contained in the resin of opium poppy seeds; *Semi-synthetic opioids* which are synthesized from natural opiates, such as Oxycodone and Heroin; *Endogenous opioids like Endorphin. All of these drugs bind to* opioid receptors which are found in the central nervous system. On binding, they cause a feeling of euphoria.

In order to test the efficacy of the Camouflaged Endorphin we possess an excellent model in the form of 'Rouén's depressive mice'; have you heard of them?" Ben and Lucia did, but Debbie did not and therefore John said: "Rouén's depressive mice are used extensively for the study of anti-depressant medications in general. This strain of mice was developed by a group of scientists from the Neuropharmacology department of the University of Rouén, France. For that, normal mice were subjected to two selection tests:

The first selection test was the "tail suspension test." In this test, mice were tied by their tails with their heads down for 6 minutes. During this suspension time the mice twisted back and forth for several seconds each time in an effort to extricate themselves. The lengths of the twisting periods during a 6 minute suspension time were summed up. The more passive, submissive mice, which exhibited the longest period of motionless despair, were selected. The depressive trait was further selected by subjecting the passive "veterans" from the first test to a second one—the "forced swimming" test: they were placed in an aquarium full of water in which they swam and twisted several times during their immersion period in the hope of getting back to "safe land"; while at other times they just floated helplessly. The most passive mice were selected again and allowed to breed. By about the twelfth generation, the trait of depression was finally perpetuated unchanged. The "Depressed Rouén mice" exhibited a behavior comparable to that of depressed human patients. They consumed much smaller quantities of a sugar solution, (which for them is very pleasurable) than normal mice. This behavior is similar to the "Anhedonistic behavior" (lack of interest in pleasure) that is exhibited by depressed persons. I want you to know that these tests, per-se, did not harm the mice, but we cannot ignore the fact that the selection processes employed in Rouén created mice that were going to live in despair and misery all their lives . . . About a year ago I wrote to the scientists in Rouén and received from them five male and ten females which have multiplied in our animal house ever since. Now, as is customary in the end of my lectures I will allow time for questions. Do you have any questions that you would like to ask"?

None had and John said: "Since the names of the materials that will "star" in our project are long, we will use for them the following abbreviations:

1. "Normal" Endorphin—**End**
2. "Truncated" (negative control) Endorphin—**TrEnd**
3. "Camouflaged" Endorphin – **C-End**
4. "Camouflaged" "Truncated" (negative control) Endorphin – **C-TrEnd.**

The scientists nodded their heads in agreement, but then Ben said: "I have an important abbreviation to add: I – C – D—End of our study." John pretended to be hurt at Ben's flippant addition and then laughed together with his colleagues.

John ended their first meeting and said: "OK then, enough of words. Let the action begin"!

4

Year 2013

Following John's exposition of the Endorphin project, Ben put Moira's picture on his desk after first proudly showing it to Debbie and Lucia. Then He started to search in all the medical and biological databases for scientific papers that might be dealing with the cloning of the Endorphin gene. He also examined various patent databases to see if there might be a drug company or a research lab that had already issued a patent on the production of Endorphin by genetic engineering. He also found a listing of the Endorphin's DNA sequence in the huge database of the Human Genome Project plus a listing of Endorphin's amino acid sequence.

After two days of search, Ben went to John's office and said: "John, I feel quite confident that the cloning of Endorphin and its production in bacteria will be very simple. Fortunately, nobody had ever cloned Endorphin till now, so that we will not be hampered by previous patents."

John said: "Excellent, Ben. When I wrote my grant-proposal to the National Institute of Mental Health (NIMH), I submitted a patent request to Harvard's office of technology that deals with such matters for Harvard's scientists and asked them to perform a patent search for possible competitors. Still I am happy for your additional checking of the patent situation. Now, if you want, let us invite Debbie and Lucia so that you can tell us how you plan to clone Endorphin and how to synthesize it." Ben agreed and John invited Debbie and Lucia to his office. In the meeting, John sat near Debbie and felt the stirrings of a sexual desire that he had not felt for quite some time.

Ben said: "People who are not familiar with biology, regard "genetic engineers" with great respect thinking that their work is nothing short of a miracle and that it can be performed only by geniuses. This is certainly not true! The genetic engineering technics that had been developed by many scientists are so brilliant and yet so simple that any high-school kid could perform them, provided he had a set of instructions and the necessary reagents and equipment. As you know, most of the proteins produced by genetic engineering (also called "recombinant proteins"), are produced in E. coli bacteria which multiply every 20 minutes. As a result of this short generation time, It is possible to produce in a few days many kilograms of genetically engineered bacteria in fermentors. Recombinant proteins can also be produced in cultures of animal cells, yeasts, insects and plants. They were even secreted into the milk of a ewe whose mother had been artificially inseminated with an egg containing a gene for a desired recombinant protein.

This is how we will proceed: First and most importantly, we will purchase all the necessary biological reagents that we will need: reagents for extracting DNA, deoxyribonucleotide tri-phosphates that are the building blocks of DNA, a cloning plasmid[8], various DNA synthesizing, cutting and ligating (connecting) enzymes, a radioactive kit for the quantitation of Endorphin, bacterial growth media, etc. Then we will isolate the Endorphin DNA gene from DNA extracted from human tissue culture cells and will replicate it in a Polymerase Chain Reaction (PCR) machine to billions of copies. One half of the synthesized Endorphin gene copies will be "truncated" by cutting 12 bases (equal to four amino acids) from one of their ends to yield truncated TrEnd DNA molecules. Both the End and the TrEnd DNA molecules will be inserted into cloning plasmid vectors by cutting—and ligating enzymes. The vectors containing the Endorphin genes will be inserted into E. coli bacteria by a method called "electroporation": the plasmid vector and target bacteria will be placed together in an electrical cell which will be "bombed" by a current of several hundred volts. This process will

---

[8] **A plasmid is a relatively small** DNA molecule that occurs naturally in bacteria and can replicate in them independently of the whole E. coli DNA. They are double stranded and, in many cases, circular. Plasmids used in genetic engineering are called vectors and are commercially available. A selected cloned gene that needs to be replicated, is inserted into copies of the plasmid which are, in turn, transferred into bacteria.

push the DNA vectors forcefully into the target E. coli bacteria. The "bombed" bacteria will be seeded onto bacterial agar plates which will contain an antibiotic that will allow only the End—and TrEnd-containing bacteria to grow into visible colonies. Some of these colonies from the agar plates will be randomly chosen and will be grown in broth cultures. These cultures will be tested for their content of End and TrEnd molecules with the radioactive quantitation kit. The colony that will produce the largest concentration of End or TrEnd molecules will be grown and divided into many portions which will be frozen for future cultivations. The plasmid vector that we will use will cause all the Endorphin produced inside the engineered bacteria to leak out during bacterial growth to the growth medium. To obtain the culture fluid with its Endorphins, the bacteria will be sedimented down in a centrifuge and discarded. The Endorphins left in the bacteria-free broth will be isolated away from the rest of the broth components by protein purification technics.

When Ben finished his description, John said: "Thank you Ben for your excellent presentation. Let us hope that you will have a smooth sailing throughout your cloning and Endorphin isolation work. I use this "sailing" form of blessing, since we live in a major shipping city . . .

5

Year 2013

In one of their weekly staff meetings, John said: "Some time ago I told you that I will describe this "camouflaging" thing to you. We need to camouflage Endorphin so that it will be able to cross the blood-brain-barrier and enter the brain.

First, what is the Blood-Brain Barrier? I am sure that you are all familiar with the term, but I like to hear myself lecture . . . The brain is the ruler of the human body and is the most complex and the most vulnerable of all organs. As a result, it sends its instructions from a well-secured region—the thick bony skull. The Blood-Brain Barrier (which I will henceforth abbreviate to B.B.B.) is an additional efficient internal security system. The B.B.B controls everything that enters the brain and prevents the inflow of viruses, bacteria and various undesirable or unnecessary materials.

The B.B.B. was discovered at the end of the 19th century by the German bacteriologist Paul Ehrlich who won a Nobel Prize for Medicine or Physiology in 1908 for his many contributions to Microbiology and Medicine. Dr. Ehrlich found that when he injected various dyes into animals, the dyes disseminated throughout the blood and stained all their tissues except for the brain which was not stained. Ehrlich wrongly hypothesized that the brain possesses low affinity for the injected dyes. One of Ehrlich's students performed the other half of the experiment: he injected the dyes into the brain and found that only brain tissues were stained and not any body tissues. He, rightly, came to the conclusion that the dye, because of some barrier, could not enter from the brain to the body and vice versa.

The whole body, including the brain, is fed by a network of arteries out of which branch thinner and thinner blood arterioles and blood capillaries. The walls of blood capillaries are made of a single layer of endothelial cells that touch each other like tiles on a roof. In the connecting spaces between the endothelial cells of the capillaries there are gaps called 'intersections' through which blood cells and nutrient materials can pass from the blood to the body tissues and back. However, these intersections in the brain are blocked by net-like protein fibers which form the B.B.B. and prevent free in-and-out flow of materials from the capillaries into brain tissues.

Unfortunately, among the materials that cannot enter into the brain are important drugs for the treatment of various brain diseases, including tumors. In order to cross the B.B.B,. drugs must possess a molecular weight smaller than 400 Daltons and to be hydrophobic (that is, to be electrically uncharged). Hydrophobic molecules (which can dissolve in fatty substances) can pass through the

B.B.B. since the walls of all cells in the body (including brain cells and the blood capillaries of the B.B.B) are made of a double lipid layer and will allow the infiltration of hydrophopic molecules. Non-hydrophobic nutrients that are required for the maintenance of the brain can still enter brain tissues through specific nutrient receptors studded in the membranes of all the brain's blood capillaries.

To allow non-hydrophobic, electrically charged drugs to cross the B.B.B., scientists have developed several technics to "sneak" them through. The best and most used technic is the "camouflaging" technic that we are going to use—electrically charged impassable drugs such as our Endorphin are bound to a fatty or hydrophobic (uncharged) carrier molecule and will thus "fool" the B.B.B. This method is also called the "Trojan horse" method after the mythological gigantic wooden horse in Homer's "Odyssey" in which the besieging Greek soldiers hid and the rest of the army sailed away. The jubilant Trojans, thinking that they finally won, breached a large entrance through their defending walls and dragged the horse inside the city to serve as a monument to their victory. At night, the Greek soldiers sneaked out from the wooden horse and conquered the city.

I will camouflage Endorphin by a chemical reaction invented by a scientist called Wei-Chiang Shen. According to his method, the charged impassable drug is combined with a lipid molecule called palmitoyl-N-epsilon-maleimido-l-lysine (PNML). After this camouflaging, we will be able to administer it to Rouén's depressed mice to test its efficacy.

6

Year 2013

John met Lucia every Thursday to discuss her progress in the second project of the lab and to plan the experiments for the next week. When they finished one such meeting, John said: "Luce, tell me something—what is your opinion of Debbie? You two already had a good chance to get acquainted, right?" Lucia understood the real reason behind John's question and said: "Debbie is still new to research, but I am quite sure that she will soon prove to be a very good scientist. If I may gossip a little, I know that she is not married (John knew that already from Debbie's Curriculum Vitae) and that she does not have a boyfriend at the moment, which is rather surprising for such a beautiful girl."

Leaving John's office, Lucia reflected: "Debbie is very sweet and Ben is also very nice. These new 'acquisitions' to the lab should add new vitality and motivation to our work. The Endorphin project will soon take me away from my current work that involves organic syntheses with strong chemicals that affect my Asthma in spite of my use of the chemical fume hood during syntheses and my Ventolin inhaler. I have a feeling that Debbie may be a suitable girlfriend for John in spite of their age difference. I will try to act as a matchmaker between them since I believe that both are interested in each other. Debbie even asked me, blushingly one day, if I know whether John is now in a relationship. I know that John feels that lecturers and thesis supervisors should not invite their students to dates. Therefore it will be a slow job, requiring my utmost tact. My best approach would be to enlist Ben and I am sure that he will join ranks with me."

True to her resolve, Lucia invited Ben to coffee in the kitchen near the lab. They conferred at some length and then both of them returned to the lab. Ben immediately went to his office and phoned Moira.

Later in the afternoon, Ben entered John's office and said: "John, I hope that you will not be cross with me for what I am about to say. I dare say it, because I believe that we are friends and not just colleagues: I think that Debbie has a "crush" on you! Whenever you speak with her she blushes and later makes some silly mistakes at work. In my opinion, not only do I think that the girl in love with you, but I also think that you are too. I can feel an undercurrent of sexual attraction between you that is so thick that one can almost cut it with a knife! Do the right thing for both of you and ask her to a date! Moira wanted to try to fix you up with some of her eligible new friends at work, but here you have a better "find" right under your nose!"

John opened his eyes in wonder and said: "Are you sure Ben? I am, indeed, strongly attracted to her. But, you may be mistaken about her feelings. Perhaps she blushes because she is simply in awe of her thesis-adviser? If I ask her out and she refuses, it will be difficult for both of us to go on working together. Alternatively, if she accepts, I may come under heavy criticism from my colleagues when they will hear about it. Worse still, I am much older and, therefore, may be unsuitable for her."

"Nonsense," said Ben. "Lucia also agrees with me that Debbie is very interested in you and that you suit each other perfectly. She suggested and I agreed that Moira and I will invite all the lab's people including Lucia's husband, Tony, to dinner at our place this coming Saturday. On Friday, Lucia will say that she and Tony, unexpectedly, have to baby-sit with their grandson and cannot come. This will give you a chance to meet Debbie under sociable circumstances. Debbie does not possess a car so that you can drive her to our home and ask her for a date when you bring her back to her apartment. If she refuses to go out with you, which I doubt, you can ask her to keep it quiet between you two and that you promise her that her decline of your invitation will not affect your mutual work relations even one whit."

John sat completely overwhelmed and said: "Why, you sneaky matchmakers! A fine ploy you concocted behind my back! I think I will sack you both!"' and then he said: "Please Ben, give me some time to think about it."

"No way", said Ben. "I spoke with Debbie a few minutes ago and she had already accepted and knows that you are going to pick her up on your way to dinner. I don't want to let the current situation between you remain unresolved since it may endanger the success of our project." John sighed and accepted the inevitable.

On Saturday John had a hair-cut, bought two bottles of expensive boutique California wine and drove in the evening to pick up Debbie. On the short way to dinner they barely had time to talk and besides, John was a little tongue-tied sitting next to the dolled-up, beautiful Debbie. When they arrived at Ben's and Moira's place, both of them breathed a little easier since the energetic Moira chatted and drew them into the conversation. Dinner went well because of the tasty meal and excellent wine. After dinner John drove Debbie to her apartment and accompanied her to the door. For a second he almost asked her to a date, but "chickened out" and just said good-bye. All the way back to his apartment, he chastised himself for his cowardly behavior and already started to compose an apologetic response to Ben and Lucia in answer to their impending questions on Monday.

Debbie locked her door disappointedly and waited near the door hoping that John might still knock. Then she drank a glass of water, went to bed and thought:

"I was hoping that John will ask me for a date to-night. I have a feeling that he wanted to, but held back. I am beginning to think that I made a mistake coming to his lab . . . I chose to work with him hoping to make him love me and to spend the all my life with him. Until now I have always succeeded in charming whomever I wanted. But, they were not venerable university professors . . .

If my mute courting will not succeed, I would try to transfer to another lab, but it will be very difficult. I feel alive only when I am near him . . .

Debbie shook her head sadly and fell asleep, dreaming of John.

7

Year 2013

While Ben and Debbie worked on the production of Endorphin, John continued to prepare his lectures for his new course and to teach in his present one. Once a week they all met so that Ben and Debbie could report on their progress, if any. Three days after their last meeting, Ben and Debbie entered John's office. John saw their faces and said eagerly: "Come on, give!"

Ben made a victory sign with his fingers, smiled and said: "I am happy to tell you that we are progressing quite nicely. Debbie, please show John the results of the quantitation tests for Endorphin that you performed on broth samples from the engineered E. coli colonies that we picked from the agar plates."

John looked at Debbie's notebook and whistled in appreciation, saying: "Wow, I can see that there are several broth samples from both the End and TrEnd colonies that contain a lot of material. Good, Good! " and then he said: "Ben and Debbie, your next obvious step would be to take the best End—and TrEnd—producing colony, grow its bacteria to large volumes, collect the culture fluids and purify the End and TrEnd molecules for me to camouflage. To speed up the work I will release Lucia from her present project to help you."

Ben answered:" sure thing, boss, thy wish shall be done!" and he bowed deeply three times . . .

The scientists left John's office and Debbie thought:

"Immersed in work, I manage to drive away all thoughts of John. But, whenever we sit in a meeting, I sense an attraction between us and feel miserable that it is not consummated. I understand that it is difficult for him to ask me to a date, being older and my thesis supervisor. But, if he soon won't make a move soon, I will ask him to a "semi-date" . . . I will pretend that I don't ski and ask him instruct me, saying that I heard that he had already instructed John. If he agrees, during the instruction I will pretend to slip and will stumble into his arms for support. I hope that this will break the ice, or more correctly, the snow between us" Then the lovelorn girl sighed and went back to work.

Two weeks after the start of the Endorphin isolation and purification experiments, Ben, Debbie and Lucia entered John's office and Ben said: "John, we are happy to tell you that we have made additional good progress! I did not realize how good Debbie, Lucia and I can be . . . We have succeeded in developing a simple yet efficient isolation and purification procedure for both the End and Tr-End molecules on a Cation exchange column. We tested both isolated Endorphins by the

SEC-HPLC[9] method and found them to be about 98% pure."

John shook his head sadly and said: "Ouch! That's not so good. Now I will have to stop preparing my course and dirty my own hands in the lab" and then he burst in a false, thin, falsetto laughter . . . Ben grimaced at John's feeble joke and theatricals and finally all joined John – hilarity and hearty laughter are very infectious!

Next day, John started his camouflage work. He added either End or TrEnd to tubes containing PNML (the lipidizing palmitoyl-N-epsilon-maleimido-l-lysine molecule) and incubated them in a 37°C waterbath for three hours. Next, he analyzed each mixture separately on a SEC-HPLC column to see if the binding was successful. The column showed 3 peaks: free End or TrEnd (depending on the analyzed reaction), Camouflaged-End or Camouflaged-TrEnd and free PNML lipid molecules (not all the End or TrEnd molecules combined with the lipidizing PNML). John showed the results to his colleagues and said:

"Dear colleagues, now it is your turn to develop a method to isolate the camouflaged C-End or the C-TrEnd molecules from the reaction mixtures."

"Ha," said Ben with a conceited smile: "Don't worry John; it is going to be a piece of cake! There are several techniques that I plan to try and I am sure that at least

---

9   **SEC-HPLC** – Size Exclusion High Pressure Liquid Chromatography is a method that separates molecules from a mixture according to their size and determines their degree of purity.

one or two of them are going to work." This braggadocio was so out of character for the generally mild-mannered Ben, that everyone looked askance at him. They finally understood when he started to laugh uproariously in falsetto, imitating John's previous tomfoolery and laughed together with him . . . The scientists were so happy with their successes, that flippancy and happy laughter came easily to them these days . . .

A week later, the three scientists came back to John with results: They obtained isolated pure C-End and C-TrEnd molecules after running the camouflaging mixtures on a column called "Hydrophobic Interaction" column. Further analyses of the isolated C-End—and C-TrEnd in an analytical instrument called Mass Spectrometer confirmed their identity and purity. The work for that day stopped (it was already late in the afternoon anyway). Since a very important milestone has been reached, John invited the team for Pizza and beer. He also invited all the lab's people including Ben's and Lucia's spouses to a posh sea food restaurant in the Brigham circle section of Boston for the coming Saturday night.

8

Year 2013

On April 15th, a very important date in the history of mankind, John and his colleagues started a crucial experiment designed to test the efficacy of Endorphin in mice. Testing was to be performed by feeding depressive Rouén mice with C-End or C-TrEnd solutions and then submitting them to the "tail suspension" test. On the day before the experiment, John taught Ben and Debbie how to perform the test: how to tie mice to inclined poles and to register the twitching time lengths of the hung mice with the sort of clock used by competing chess players. These clocks were set to ring at the end of 6 minutes.

Before the end of the day's work, John addressed his team haltingly: "I am about to say something that may astound you: I am a rational scientist, but ever since I have started doing research, I carry a rabbit's foot in my pocket – the left hind foot of a rabbit shot in a graveyard in the new moon. I bought this amulet in a Woodoo shop in New-Orleans many years ago. I don't know if it "works", but the fact is that ever since buying the amulet I have never failed in any scientific experiment that I performed . . . If you yourselves have any such "scientific" implements that might draw "good energies" into the lab, can you bring them to to-morrow's crucial experiment?" John expected some heavy Joshing at his expense, but to his relief none came. Moreover, Lucia said: "I never take off the crucifix that I wear" and John said: "I carry a silver horse-shoe in my key-ring against evil eye and interestingly, I first met Moira, my lovely Irish girl for the first time on the very same day that I bought it, so there you are." Lastly Debbie said: "I wear a "Hamsa" necklace that was given to me by my grand-mother. Hamsa is a good luck amulet in the form of a palm of a hand and stands for the five books of the Pentateuch in the Old Testament." Awkwardly John summarized their discussion by saying: "Fine, we are well equipped for to-morrow's experiment!"

On the day of the test, the scientists prepared six tubes with different colored stickers and filled them with sugar solutions. Then they added End or C-End or C-TrEnd to the tubes so that each tube contained the type and amount of material that they wanted to administer in each 0.5 milliliter volume. Next, they prepared three sub-sets of the six tubes with the same six materials—one for each scientist.

The materials and amounts that were to be administered to the mice in 0.5 milliliter volumes were as follows:

1. microgram End (control – not supposed to work because of the blood-brain-barrier) – brown sticker
2. 5 microgram End (control – not supposed to work because of the blood-brain-barrier) – Red sticker
3. 1 microgram C-End (hopefully should work) – yellow sticker
4. 5 microgram C-End (hopefully should work) – blue sticker
5. 1 microgram C-TrEnd (control – presumably should not work because it is damaged) – white sticker
6. 5 microgram C-TrEnd (control – presumably should not work because it is damaged) – green sticker

Lucia prepared 3 mouse cages, each containing randomly chosen six male and female Rouén mice and painted their backs with six colored markers according to the stickers listed above. Administration of the various tested solutions to the mice was to be performed by filling syringes with 0.5 milliliter volumes and feeding each color-coded mouse with the corresponding color-coded solution. Each mouse was transferred after feeding to a second empty cage which eventually housed six differently colored fed mice for each scientist.

Prior to feeding, John, Ben and Debbie tested the 6-minute basal-twitching-times of the mice. This was going to serve as the control zero time. Each scientist wrote the control twitching time results of his mice in a column marked "0 hr" in a table that they prepared beforehand,

At the 0.5 hour time-point since feeding, the scientists measured the twitching times of their mice, calculated the average of the twitching times of all three mice of the same color (John's, Ben's and Debbie's) and wrote the mean results in a common table. The average results obtained from the 0 and 0.5 hour measurements are presented in Table 1 below.

Table 1. Lengths of the twitching times of Rouén depressed mice at 0 hr and 0.5 hrs post feeding with End, C-End and C-TrEnd

Material fed and its amount (micrograms)	Time Length of twitching (seconds)* for the various testing times since feeding							
	0 hr before feeding	0.5 hr	1 hr	4 hr	12 hr	22 hr	26 hr	30 hr
End 1	29	30						
End 5	28	29						
C-End 1	28	43						
C-End 5	32	60						
C-TrEnd 1	35	84						
C-TrEnd 5	29	97						

*) The values for the time lengths of twitching are the average of 3 mice from the same color

The scientists looked at the 0.5 hr results in table 1 with rising hopes: The mice fed with 1—and 5-microgram of both C-End and C-TrEnd showed an increase in their twitching times relative to the non-camouflaged 1—and 5—milligram End.

John said: "The results look promising. If they will hold and even improve, I will be able to say that our "magical scientific amulets" worked . . . So far, so good. But before we start to celebrate, let us wait for additional testing times since "a single cuckoo does not herald spring." It is perplexing, though, that C-TrEnd, which was supposed to serve as a negative control, appears to work even better than whole, untruncated, C-End! In addition, in case you have not noticed, there is one additional good omen – depressed Rouén male mice are apathetic and only rarely mate with the females; but those mice treated with camouflaged C-End and C-TrEnd started to sniff the females in their cages, whereas those fed with uncamouflaged End remained apathetic as before!"

At the one hour time-point, the scientists measured the twitching times again. The averaged calculated results are presented in Table 2.

Table 2. Lengths of the twitching times of Rouén depressed mice at 0 hr, 0.5—and 1 hrs post feeding with End, C-End and C-TrEnd

Material fed and its amount (micrograms)	Time Length of twitching (seconds)* for the various testing times since feeding							
	0 hr before feeding	0.5 hr	1 hr	4 hr	12 hr	22 hr	26 hr	30 hr
End 1	29	30	32					
End 5	28	29	25					
C-End 1	28	43	80					
C-End 5	32	60	90					
C-TrEnd 1	35	84	135					
C-TrEnd 5	29	97	150					

*) The values for the time lengths of twitching are the average of 3 mice from the same color

The scientists looked eagerly at the averaged one hour results and their joy was boundless! – They cheered enthusiastically, as if at the sight of an especially pleasing "dunk" by a Celtics' Forward! The trend that they started to see at 0.5 hours continued to strengthen and they could also see that the C-End and C-TrEnd males mated energetically with the females in their cages!

John happily started a round of hugging and cheek-kissing starting with Ben and Lucia. When he came to Debbie he hesitated a little, but then he held her waist gingerly planning to kiss her cheek. However Debbie, grasping her chance, moved her face as if by mistake and their lips met! Automatically John's arms tightened around her and he kissed her ardently, waiting for a rebuke which did not come . . . When they "came back for air", John and Debbie looked at each other lovingly. Debbie sighed happily and said: "John, dearest, what took you so long! I have waited so long for your kiss and have almost given up on you!"

John answered enthusiastically: "Debbie, my love, I could not believe that a lovely girl like you would even consider loving an older, chubby person like me!" Suddenly they became aware of their surroundings and looked with embarrassment at Ben and Lucia who raised their thumbs in approval . . .

Since the scientists had three free hours to spend until the next measurement, they went to lunch, with John and Debbie arm in arm. They chatted happily throughout lunch, discussing the 2 momentous events that just happened, ignoring the eyes of all the guests who watched them with interest.

On coming back to the lab, the new lovers went to John's office. They kissed again passionately and decided to go to John's house at the end of the day. Debbie came out of the office with a light step and a flushed and happy face. Ben and Debbie pretended to work, stealing a peek at Debbie's happy face from time to time and winked discreetly at each other.

The 4 hour measurement came and its results are presented in Table 3.

Table 3. Lengths of the twitching times of Rouén depressed mice at 0.5-, 1—and 4 hrs post feeding with End, C-End and C-TrEnd

Material fed and its amount (micrograms)	Time Length of twitching (seconds)* for the various testing times since feeding							
	0 hr before feeding	0.5 hr	1 hr	4 hr	12 hr	22 hr	26 hr	30 hr
End 1	29	30	32	25				
End 5	28	29	25	26				
C-End 1	28	43	80	150				
C-End 5	32	60	90	167				
C-TrEnd 1	35	84	135	190				
C-TrEnd 5	29	97	150	210				

*) The values for the time lengths of twitching are the average of 3 mice from the same color

Both camouflaged C-End and C-Trend, but not End, at both the 1—and 5 microgram amounts, continued to work marvelously with C-TrEnd leading the field.

The scientists went home for an 8-hour break till the 12th hour measurement at 10 PM. The happy couple, John and Debbie, arrived at John's apartment. As soon as they closed the door behind them, they clung and kissed eagerly, hastily helping each other to remove their clothes and with yearning sighs stumbled to bed, diving into a sea of love and fulfillment. All evening and early night they celebrated their new love, intimately learning to know each other's body, intimate biography and soul.

Marvelously satiated they met Ben and Lucia for the 12th hour measurements and then, on the next day, continued with the 22hr-, 26hr—and 30hr—measurements. The final results of the efficacy testing experiment are summarized in the final table, table 4:

Table 4. Lengths of twitching times of Rouén depressed mice at various times since their feeding with End, C-End and C-TrEnd

Material fed and its amount (micrograms)	Time Length of twitching (seconds)* for the various testing times							
	0 hr before feeding	0.5 hr	1 hr	4 hr	12 hr	22 hr	26 hr	30 hr
End 1	29	30	32	25	22	22	25	28
End 5	28	29	25	26	27	23	28	25
C-End 1	28	43	80	150	140	101	70	30
C-End 5	32	60	90	167	159	92	79	41
C-TrEnd 1	35	84	135	190	185	109	99	80
C-TrEnd 5	29	97	150	210	205	130	119	92

*) The values for the time length of twitching is the average of 3 mice from the same color

The doubly happy John summarized the results of the experiment in a lecturer's pedagogic tone: "As you know, it is not always possible to predict the outcome of biological experiments. I was quite sure that the truncated C-TrEnd will not work and would serve as a negative control material. To my surprise, it worked even better than undamaged C-End! Apparently, the piece of Endorphin that we cut, is not essential to Endorphin's activity and perhaps it even partly inhibited its action. Notice also that both concentrations of C-TrEnd and C-End exerted their action throughout more than 24 hours. This means that they possess very useful Pharmacokinetics[10] (at least in Mice, and hopefully also

---

[10]   **Pharmacokinetics**-Pharmacokinetics is the study of the absorption and distribution of an administered drug in the body.

in Men) – i.e., they are only slowly eliminated from the body. As a result, my prediction is that just a single administration of the drug to humans per day should suffice.

Now let us consider how to proceed. For the immediate future we have to cross three main milestones:

Will the Endorphin be addictive? This point will be first tested in mice.

Will the C-TrEnd and/or C-End work successfully also in humans? I am fairly confident that it will since the biochemistries and physiologies of mice and men are similar.

Will the C-TrEnd and C-End be addictive in humans? It is known that persons who enjoy an Endorphin's "runners' high" when they jog or train in a fitness club find it difficult, though not impossible, to stop exercising."

In the evening after the end of the efficacy experiment John said: "Debbie my love, we have known each other for two months and for several hours only as lovers. Still, I would like to offer you to move in with me. Please think about my offer." Debbie looked adoringly at John and immediately agreed. Thus started a wonderful partnership between them in research, love, marriage and the raising of their children which was destined to last for many years.

Author's note: Copies of the tables of the efficacy experiment in Rouén mice can be found in SOMA museums which had been established in major cities across the world.

9

Year 2013

A few days after the Endorphin's successful efficacy test in mice, John invited his colleagues to a meeting and said: "Dear friends, our next and very important step will be to test whether C-TrEnd or C-End will induce addiction in mice after prolonged use. This is how we will run the experiment: we will prepare two regular cages which will house depressed Rouén mice and will contain food pellets and water with either C-End or C-TrEnd. The mice will live in these cages for four weeks in order to allow them to develop addiction to the Endorphins if, god forbid, they will induce it. I have asked the University's machine shop to prepare for us a special "torture" cage according to my design: one half of the floor in the cage is a heat-resistant asbestos plate, whereas the other half is made of a stainless steel heating plate controlled by a thermostat. At the far end the wall, adjacent to the heating plate, we will hang a water-trough which will contain a solution of 5 microgram per milliliter of C-End or C-TrEnd, during the actual addiction test.

At the end of a 4 weeks' "habituation" period we will remove the drugs from the 2 "regular" cages and replace them with water without drug for three additional days in order to create a "yen" for the Endorphins. Next, we will transfer one C-End or C-TrEnd habituated mouse at a time to the addiction-testing "torture" cage whose heating plate will be turned on to 60° degrees Centigrade. The habituated mouse will run from the harmless asbestos plate towards the Endorphin-containing trough at the far end of the cage. If the mouse had developed addiction to either the C-End or C-TrEnd, it will persevere and will drink from the C-End or C-Trend water in-spite of the heat under its paws. If it is not addicted, it will run back to the asbestos plate and will give up any effort after a few tries to enjoy its regular "fix".

On the night before the addiction test, John lay awake in bed, with success and failure scenarios flashing back and forth in his mind. When he finally fell asleep, he dreamed of human-faced mice that poked their tongues at him in derision.

Next day, bleary-eyed and tense and surrounded by his colleagues, John picked up one mouse from the C-End habituated group and placed it in the "torture cage." The mouse quickly ran from the asbestos half to the C-End trough. At first it was taken back by the heat, but persevered and drank, raising one paw and another as a man on the beach crossing a particularly hot patch of sand. After the drinking its fill, the mouse ran back to the asbestos plate, lied on its back and licked its burned paws. The same scenario repeated itself with 2 additional mice. The merciful Debbie and Lucia picked the poor mice and spread analgesic ointment on their paws. The gloomy scientists stood still, knowing that the future of the project is now rather uncertain.

John said in an anguished voice: "Ah, I knew it, I knew it! Things went too smoothly until now – it was too good to be true!"

With considerably reduced hopes John started to test the C-TrEnd habituated mice. In seconds the scientists' mood changed: the first C-TrEnd mouse ran "happily" towards the trough, stepped on the heating plate and immediately made a hasty retreat back to the "safe" asbestos plate. A few seconds later it tried again and immediately retreated, as before. It crouched on the asbestos half with "a disappointed face" (this is probably what the scientists would have identified if they had been able to read the body—and "face" language of mice).

With shaking hands John repeated the experiment with two additional mice, obtaining the same result. The level of happiness rose from one mouse test to the other! John grabbed Debbie and started to waltz, humming a tune and Ben did the same with Lucia. A scientist who passed by the door of the animal facility was attracted by the mirth causing John to mumble some lame excuse for their unusual behavior . . . When they finally calmed down, John said: "Dear colleagues, by sheer luck, it seems that the small sequence that we cut from the end of the Endorphin is responsible the induction of addiction by the complete C-End peptide, in addition to its slight inhibitory action that we detected in the efficacy experiment! The results are quite clear. From now on, C-TrEnd is our only boy, or girl, if you wish!

We have made splendid breakthroughs in a very short time and this deserves celebration. Therefore, if you, Ben and Lucia, do not have any prior obligations for the coming week-end, I would like to invite you and your spouses at my expense to a resort on the beachfront of Cape Cod. Debbie, you are also invited . . . I have heard good reports about this resort from some colleague and wanted to try it for quite a while. I was told that aside from the usual resort attractions it has an excellent chef. Ben and Lucia agreed and John immediately made reservations.

The scientists and their spouses and girlfriend drove to the resort and as soon as all the couples settled in their rooms John called the scientists to a short meeting in the resort's pub. He said: "Dear colleagues, we still have some obstacles to pass: we don't know yet if humans will also respond favorably to C-TrEnd. If they will, will they, unlike mice, become addicted? However, now that we have passed some important milestones, I would like to christen C-TrEnd and give it a catching and meaningful name instead of its current chemical name. The name that I thought of is "SOMA." This is the name that a British author, Aldous Huxley, gave to a mythical happiness-inducing drug that he described in a 1932 science fiction book. However, I am open to other suggestions." The scientists thought for a while and could not think of a better name. Seeing that,

John said: "No? Then it is settled. Let us raise a toast to celebrate the birth of our SOMA!

I don't want to discuss work on this weekend. This is not what we came for. I just want to say that on our immediate agenda will also be the performance of pre-clinical drug safety tests in various animals such as mice, dogs and monkeys. This is essential before FDA will let us test our SOMA in humans. For this purpose we will hire the services of a company that specializes in this type of testing and had obtained a certification from FDA. This testing will take about two to three months. Let us cross our fingers and hope for good results from the company.

Now, I would like to make an announcement: if we will succeed in our project, Harvard will get a large share of any profits accrued by selling the right to market SOMA to a pharmaceutical or biotechnological company. Part of the profits will come to me. Although I am the chief scientist and the holder of the SOMA patent, I would like to share these profits equally between the four of us." This very generous offer by John rendered the other three scientists completely speechless. They immediately thanked him enthusiastically, but John waved aside their thanks saying that they deserved it!

Then Ben "piped": "Hey, Hey, hold it; this is not fair – Lucia and I will get only one quarter each, while you and Debbie after you get married, will have two quarters!" After Ben dropped his "bomb", John stole a glance at Debbie who blushed. But, Ben quickly said: "Hey, Hey, I was kidding, I was kidding. I simply tried to promote for you the level of your relationship!" . . .

The scientists set a time for dinner and Ben and Lucia hurried back to their rooms to relate the important news to their spouses.

Lucia related the news to Tony and said: "what a generous boss I have. He could have kept all the profits from the SOMA to himself. Instead, he decided to share it equally with us. If the SOMA will succeed, it will greatly improve our financial situation."

Tony rejoiced too, but being a practical person, said: "Luce, let us wait until the SOMA is certified before we go to the bank to cash on its success. Meanwhile, try to see if you could gently convince John to anchor his promise in a legal contract? . . ."

Ben told Moira what happened in the meeting and she said happily: "Why, this is certainly in line with what I already know about John. If the drug would work, we would be able carry out our plans to have children earlier than we thought!"

10

Year 2013

On August 15th, the contractor pre-clinical testing company finished its work and sent the results to John. He assembled his team and said: "dear friends, in the past months we have obtained a very pure product which does not contain any bacterial or chemical contaminants. I have before me the results of the pre-clinical safety study that the contract company did for us, that I will let soon let you read. Their verdict was that the SOMA was, unequivocally, safe to all the species of animals that they tested. The animals did not exhibit any toxic damage even after a long administration of the SOMA and a pathological examination of their organs did not reveal any abnormality. Moreover, the offspring of SOMA-treated mice did not reveal any hereditary defects. The conclusion of Dr. Walton, the experienced manager of the company, was that the SOMA passed all safety tests with flying colors. Therefore, FDA is certain to permit us to perform clinical experiments in human patients. However, in order to obtain such permission, I will have to write a very extensive document called IND application – short for "Investigational New Drug Application"—and submit it to FDA for approval. It will contain all the results of the pre-clinical study company, all our data relating to the development and production of the SOMA and analytical data proving its quality and purity. As a result, I will be busy for some weeks. In the meantime I want you to produce more SOMA batches for the coming clinical trials in humans on the assumption that FDA will eventually allow it.

Before testing human subjects, I plan to test the safety and efficacy of the SOMA on myself, somewhat illegally. I don't think that it will harm me because we know from the pre-clinical safety report that the SOMA was safe to all species of animals tested. Even monkeys, which are close to us genetically, did not exhibit any untoward reaction. They chatted a lot and seemed to be happy. I have slowly weaned myself from Cipramil during the last two months so that I can try the SOMA on myself both for safety and for efficacy. The human medical research history of the 18th and 19th centuries abounds with stories of brave scientists or physicians who infected themselves with dangerous bacteria or viruses in order to test the efficacy of drugs or vaccines that they have developed. Some of them actually did pay the ultimate price for their daring. But I, on the other hand, because of our successful pre-clinical results, feel quite confident that no harm will come to me."

Debbie tried to dissuade John from performing this trial but, worriedly, ceased trying when she saw that he was adamant. John's colleagues mulled over his decision and then Ben said: "Listen John, I would like to join you in this" and a minute later Lucia and Debbie also clamored for the right to join him.

John said: "Dear friends, I am touched by your volunteering; but, please, take a minute to be sure. I will not take it amiss if any of you backs off." All three insisted on participation until John finally agreed but said: "Very well then. Let us go home now and do it to-night. I will be the first guinea pig and Debbie will watch over me, and at the very first sign of any irregularity will call an ambulance to take me to Harvard's Health Services which are open 24 hours. Ben and Lucia, if everything will be well after an hour or two, I will call you and give you clearance to take the SOMA. If you want, you can also take an additional dose also for your spouses if it will work and they would also like to try it after you."

The scientists prepared bottles containing 5 milligram portions of SOMA solution to take home (tentatively calculated to be 5000 fold stronger than the 1 microgram which worked for Rouén mice). On coming home, John and Debbie ate a light dinner and John was ready to make the plunge. Prior to drinking, John measured his blood pressure, pulse and temperature and recorded the results. His pulse was racing, but this was to be expected. Then he said: "here goes nothing" and drank, with Debbie watching over him worriedly like a hawk and trying not to show it. 15 minutes later he measured his blood pressure, pulse and his body temperature again – they remained unchanged. John and Debbie sat on the sofa hugging each other, talking quietly and watching the clock from time to time. It seemed to them that it slowed down on purpose in order to spite them . . . every few minutes Debbie asked John how he felt and he answered worriedly that he is fine, but is starting to doubt the efficacy of their invention! Debbie tried to calm him by saying that the mice took 30 minutes to react and then only slightly, and that the SOMA is probably absorbed more slowly in humans.

After 30 minutes had elapsed, John suddenly said: "My God, something is starting to happen." He measured his physiological parameters again and saw that his pulse slowed down to a normal 60 times per minute and felt that all his of worries have dissipated and were replaced by serenity and bliss! He told Debbie of his new feelings and that he does not feel any ill effects from the drug, causing her to sigh finally with relief and joy—during the first half hour she could barely breathe and was poised to dial 911 at the slightest suspicious sign . . .

John sat quietly beaming, enjoying his serenity and kissing Debbie from time-to-time. At the end of one hour he called Ben and Lucia who hovered worriedly over the phone and gave them the green light to start. Then he addressed Debbie: "Debbie my love, the SOMA works very well and I am now fairly confident that no harm will come to its drinkers. If you want, you can try it too." The trusting girl drank the SOMA and as soon as she drank, John laughed in satanic glee, saying in a changed harsh voice: "Ha, Ha, Ha, I tricked you! The SOMA released a satanic alter-ego in me like

Mr. Hyde's. Now I will make you suffer, you bitch!"
He bared his teeth, bringing them to Debbie's throat
and his pretended bite turned into a long passionate
kiss. Debbie was taken back for a second, but quickly
recovered. John laughed uproariously, but Debbie only
gave him a wan smile and finally erupted: "John, you
swine, this is no laughing matter! I was worried stiff
for you and this is how you pay me?! Don't worry! You
will pay for what you did just now! You will be my slave
every night for one week and will do all my bidding! In
addition, you will do all the house-cleaning, laundry,
the buying of groceries and the cooking all by yourself."
All that remained for John was to shut his mouth and
to nod contritely in agreement . . .

Debbie, who also started to enjoy the effects of the
SOMA, finally forgave John and they both sat on the
sofa enjoying their new state of serenity and euphoria.
Then they looked at each other, kissed again and went
to bed . . .

Around 12 PM John called Ben to ask him how he
felt and Ben enthusiastically praised the wonders of the
SOMA, adding that Moira also took the SOMA with
the same wonderful results. John received the same kind
of response when he called Lucia and Tony.

Next day, the scientists came to work radiant and
marvelously happy. They convened in John's office
and each described his or her experiences of the last 16
hours. Towards the end of the work-day their euphoria
dissipated leaving them still quiet and serene.

Around noon, Ben entered John's office and said:
"John, I want to describe a phenomenon that did not

come out in our debriefing session. I wonder whether you and Debbie also felt the same. As you know, I am still taking Seroxat that reduces libido. But, yesterday, Moira and I "celebrated" in bed just as at the start of our relationship"!

John said: "Wow! This is exactly what Debbie and I felt last night. It is possible that we are looking at an additional excellent side-effect of the SOMA. If so, what else can the SOMA do? Can it, perhaps, also strengthen the immune system which is strongly influenced by a person's mental state? Can it also deliver additional benefits?"

About 24-32 hours after taking the SOMA, the scientists became "normal" again since the SOMA had finally cleared out of their bodies. John worriedly asked each one of them if they felt an uncontrollable urge for another "fix." All said that aside from a wish to enjoy the SOMA again, they did not feel any uncontrollable need for it.

The scientists re-convened a day later and John said: "Dear partners, we have taken the SOMA just once and continued our life without any signs of addiction. However, it is still possible that we would develop addiction after long use. Heroin dependence and addiction, for example, may set in after a few times of abuse, but sometimes it may take longer. Therefore, we have to test whether the SOMA will induce drug dependence and addiction after long use. I believe that it won't, because of our mouse addiction experiment. In addition, unlike the case of Heroin that is purified from the Asian poppy plant and was not supposed, biologically, to be ingested by humans, the SOMA is essentially (in spite of its truncated state) a natural neurotransmitter of the brain. I am going to test the effect of SOMA on myself for one month to see if it induces addiction. If it does, God forbid, it will be your task to wean me."

Once again Ben, Debbie and Lucia claimed the right to join John and Ben even said: "Look John, in my opinion, if we become addicted, it will be to a wonderful drug that, apparently, does not cause any harm; so who cares if we become addicted? Since it works so well, we and all Humanity will want, anyway, to take the SOMA every day of our lives, won't we?"

John nodded in agreement but said: "You are absolutely right John. However, we need to test the possibility of addiction for 2 reasons: 1) what will happen if there will be a temporary production shortage of the SOMA or if people will run out of money to buy it – will they suffer bad withdrawal effects? 2) FDA will want proof that the SOMA is not addictive."

So the scientists entered a month-long "binge" on SOMA. Since they were free of any anxiety because of the SOMA's action, they passed their days in bliss – a state that occasionally prompted their colleagues in the Neurochemistry department to ask what is it that they are "high" on, and what is the address of their dealer . . .

At the end of the month, the team stopped taking the SOMA in a "cold turkey" manner and examined their physical and mental condition. They were, of course, less euphoric and serene relative to their SOMA period, but found that a "cold turkey" withdrawal from the SOMA was quite possible. Thus the scientists crossed another very important milestone.

Now that their fear of addiction was removed, John said: "Luckily, the SOMA is not addictive but I still want dispel another of my worries."

Ben stopped John saying: "Hey, what is the matter with you John? Are you never satisfied?"

John smiled and continued: "As you may remember from Huxley's book that I forced you to read, his SOMA had a serious flaw: it completely removed any incentive for progress and change. People in Huxley's Utopia (or more correctly, Distopia . . .) lived in a society composed of classes – Alpha, Beta and down to Epsilon. Members of each class underwent a form of differential classification as pre-planned by their intended class which was carried out by the addition of various chemicals to the gestation bottles and later by a conditioning process called "Hypnopaedia" (teaching during sleep). Both this and the SOMA made them complacent and prevented them from having any free initiative and free thinking, regardless of class. They were employed in a list of professions open only to their class. Thus, Alphas were employed in the more important jobs and Epsilons, for instance, performed only simple menial jobs. This is highly reminiscent of a passage in Homer's "Odyssey." During their sailing for home, Odysseus and his men reached an island whose citizens ate the fruit of the Lotus plant and became "happy idiots." Some of Odysseus' men also ate the fruit and forgot who they were and their wish to return home to Ithaca. They only wanted to continue their happy and "zombie-like" existence. Odysseus had to tie them by force and to carry them weeping to their ship.

Interestingly, the Buddhists and the ancient Egyptians prepared and drank an essence of the blue Lotus plant (also called the "holy Egyptian Lotus") and praised its use. Several studies have shown that an extract prepared from the Lotus plant possessed narcotic properties. By extension from the Odyssey's Lotus, what will happen to SOMA users? Will they also become so complacent and happy that they will cease to work, to strive and to exert themselves in daily life? We did not demonstrate any such tendency, but then we are highly motivated and have strong reasons to succeed for the sake of the world. Therefore, it will be important to test the SOMA's long-range psychological effects on motivation in future clinical tests.

As for our clinical studies, with our own resources we will be able carry out only limited clinical trials in humans. FDA demands the performance of very extensive double-blind clinical trials in thousands of patients before certifying any drug. Therefore, clinical testing in humans requires the enlistment of thousands of patients and scores of medical centers and hospitals. It costs more than hundred million dollars to achieve certification of every new drug and many drugs already fail at the start or in the middle of clinical trials. We will have to find a big pharmaceutical company that will be interested in our SOMA and in return for production and marketing rights will perform all the necessary extensive clinical trials required for certification.

Concerning clinical tests, let me recount to you an interesting story about the very first clinical test that, according to the Old Testament, had ever been carried out in the world: It is found in the book of Daniel." Upon saying that, John distributed Xeroxed copies of the first chapter of the book of Daniel that he had prepared some time ago for a lecture in one of his undergraduate courses:

"1:1 In the third year of the reign of Jehoiakim king of Judah came Nebuchadnezzar king of Babylon unto Jerusalem, and besieged it.

1:2 And the Lord gave Jehoiakim king of Judah into his hand, with part of the vessels of the house of God: which he carried into the land of Shinar to the house of his god; and he brought the vessels into the treasure house of his god.

1:3 And the king spake unto Ashpenaz the master of his eunuchs, that he should bring certain of the children of Israel, and of the king's seed, and of the princes;

1:4 Children in whom was no blemish, but well favoured, and skilful in all wisdom, and cunning in knowledge, and understanding science, and such as had ability in them to stand in the king's palace, and whom they might teach the learning and the tongue of the Chaldeans.

1:5 And the king appointed them a daily provision of the king's meat, and of the wine which he drank: so nourishing them three years, that at the end thereof they might stand before the king.

1:6 Now among these were of the children of Judah, Daniel, Hananiah, Mishael, and Azariah:

1:7 Unto whom the prince of the eunuchs gave names: for he gave unto Daniel the name of Belteshazzar; and to Hananiah, of Shadrach; and to Mishael, of Meshach; and to Azariah, of Abednego.

1:8 But Daniel purposed in his heart that he would not defile himself with the portion of the king's meat, nor with the wine which he drank: therefore he requested of the prince of the eunuchs that he might not defile himself.

1:9 Now God had brought Daniel into favour and tender love with the prince of the eunuchs.

1:10 And the prince of the eunuchs said unto Daniel, I fear my lord the king, who hath appointed your meat and your drink: for why should he see your faces worse liking than the children which are of your sort? then shall ye make me endanger my head to the king.

1:11 Then said Daniel to Melzar, whom the prince of the eunuchs had set over Daniel, Hananiah, Mishael, and Azariah,

1:12 Prove thy servants, I beseech thee, ten days; and let them give us pulse (all kinds of grain) to eat, and water to drink.

1:13 Then let our countenances be looked upon before thee, and the countenance of the children that eat of the portion of the king's meat: and as thou seest, deal with thy servants.

1:14 So he consented to them in this matter, and proved them ten days.

1:15 And at the end of ten days their countenances appeared fairer and fatter in flesh than all the children which did eat the portion of the king's meat.

1:16 Thus Melzar took away the portion of their meat, and the wine that they should drink; and gave them pulse.

1:17 As for these four children, God gave them knowledge and skill in all learning and wisdom: and Daniel had understanding in all visions and dreams.

1:18 Now at the end of the days that the king had said he should bring them in, then the prince of the eunuchs brought them in before Nebuchadnezzar.

1:19 And the king communed with them; and among them all was found none like Daniel, Hananiah, Mishael, and Azariah: therefore stood they before the king.

1:20 And in all matters of wisdom and understanding, that the king enquired of them, he found them ten times better than all the magicians and astrologers that were in all his realm."

"FDA and all health authorities in the world have toughened their requirements since the infamous mishap of Thalidomide in the 1960's: a German company called Grünenthal released Thalidomide for use as an effective tranquilizer and painkiller. The company claimed that Thalidomide prevents insomnia, coughs, colds, headaches and morning sickness and thousands of pregnant women in Europe took the drug. Unfortunately, it was not known at that time that drugs could pass across the placental barrier from the mother to the developing fetus and might harm it. Therefore, no safety testing was performed on pregnant animals to see if Thalidomide was harmful to their offspring. Unfortunately, Thalidomide, when taken in the first trimester, was extremely dangerous for developing fetuses and as a result, scores of thousands of babies suffering from terrible birth defects were born all over Europe. In the US, Thalidomide had only minimal distribution due to the vigilance of a FDA official named Dr. Frances Oldham Kelsey. Dr. Kelsey refused to release the drug to the American market, insisting that it required more safety testing. For her vigilance she was awarded the President's Award for Distinguished Federal Civilian Service by President John F. Kennedy.

Let me sum for you, very briefly, the steps that each new drug must successfully pass. These steps are carried out in three consecutive stages and we have already passed successfully the first two stages so I know that you are already quite familiar with them. Still, I want to discuss them up again since, as you already know . . ." His team immediately stopped him, reciting in unison: "I like to hear myself lecture . . ." and all broke out in laughter.

After they calmed down, John said: "First stage: Discovery, development and production of the drug. After production it is necessary to test the purity of the drug by using a variety of sensitive quality control tests required by health authorities. In addition, the dosage form of the drug is chosen at this stage – Inhalers, syrups, ointments, tablets, suppositories, injectible drugs, etc.

Second stage: Performance of pre-clinical testing in laboratory animals. If there is a species of an animal with a disorder similar to the human one (like our Rouén mice), it is used to test the efficacy of the drug. Next, the Pharmacokinetics of the drug are tested. The pre-clinical tests are generally performed in mice, rats, dogs and monkeys. Several safety parameters are tested: Weight-loss or gain, blood pressure, various neurological tests, the possible existence of toxic degradation products, etc. Finally, the animals are "sacrificed" (euphemism for killed . . .) and their organs are resected to identify possible tissue damage. Unfortunately, there is no escaping from this type of testing if we want to help countless human sufferers.

Stage 3: Testing safety and efficacy in patients: These tests are carried out in 4 phases and cost upward of 100 million dollars per drug:

A phase 1 Clinical safety test is carried out in 20 paid healthy human volunteers for 2 weeks with a dose that is higher than the expected therapeutic dose. In the course of this phase, the volunteers undergo a battery of tests to determine whether the drug harmed them.

A phase 2 trial is a double blind one performed on 100–200 patients, half of whom are treated with the drug and the other half with a placebo. This phase tests both efficacy and safety. If the results are satisfactory, an additional phase 2 trial is carried out with different doses of the drug in order to choose the optimal dose which is both safe and efficacious.

A phase 3 clinical trial is carried out in many medical centers with several thousand patients, again under complete double-blind conditions. If the drug is significantly more efficacious than placebo, the results of the clinical trials of phases 1, 2 and 3 are sent to the FDA in the form of a very long document called NDA (New Drug Application, not to be confused with IND). FDA studies the results and performs a close inspection of the production site and the production process. If everything is in order, it will issue a provisional marketing approval.

In phase 4, the drug company continues to monitor the results of its new drug; if no unusual side-effects are encountered, FDA finally issues a final marketing approval for the drug. It should be mentioned, however, that even after a phase 4 approval, there have been cases where FDA issued a late withdrawal demand. This happens when extensive and prolonged use of the drug revealed dangerous side-effects that were not yet apparent in the first year of its use.

Dear colleagues, after my long "treatise" you can understand why we need to produce enough SOMA for extensive clinical trials, hire a Clinical Research Organization (CRO) for testing and obtain the financial backing of a large pharmaceutical company.

A few days later, John again assembled his team and said: "protein drugs produced by genetic engineering are always much more expensive than those produced by organic chemistry. The latter are prepared from chemical raw materials which can be produced relatively cheaply in hundreds of kilograms. We do not know, as yet, what will be the lowest SOMA dose that would produce an optimal response in humans. All we know is that 5 milligrams of SOMA per day worked very well for us. If we take into account the fact that the SOMA will be taken by people once a day for life, we must come to the conclusion that the continuous use of the drug will become a very expensive habit. When a proteinaceous drug is taken by mouth, part of it is digested by enzymes in the alimentary track before it is absorbed to the blood and moves from there to the brain. Therefore, I thought of a more efficient mode of a dosage administration that will require much smaller amounts of administered SOMA per patient.

Before describing this mode to you, I want to ask you a riddle – what is it that Lucia does several times a day and I don't mean just going to the bathroom, picking her nose or washing her hands?" The team thought hard until finally Debbie said: "I know, I know! Because of her asthma, poor Luce uses her Ventolin inhaler several times a day."

John said: "Right!—give my sweet and smart Debbie two points and a cigar! We will administer the SOMA to patients directly to the lungs with an inhaler which will be filled with powdered SOMA. From the lungs, the SOMA will be absorbed without any loss directly into the blood and from thence to the brain. For this purpose we will contract the services of a company with a know-how and the suitable machines for the production of inhalers. We will ask them to freeze-dry the SOMA solutions that we will supply them, to grind the resulting dried powder into very small powder microcrystals, encase the microcrystals in lipid coats and to fill them into metered-dose inhalers. Metered dose inhalers are new sophisticated inhalers that are designed in such a way so as to deliver an exact amount of drug in each whiff. For dosage-testing we will tell the company to prepare for us inhalers that will deliver varying amounts of SOMA, from one microgram up to five thousand micrograms, in each whiff. A small digital display in the inhalers will show the number of whiffs left after each use. In order not to waste needless amounts of the SOMA, the inhalers will be adjusted to permit the delivery of only one whiff each 24 hours. This precaution will be important in case of patients with mental frailty and various other mental disorders that may not be able to keep count. All patients will be told to put the orifice of the inhalers in their mouths, purse their lips, press the activating piston to release the drug into their mouths and without opening their mouths, inhale air through their noses. We will try various dose inhalers on ourselves, one different concentration per each day, in order to determine, by consensus, which is the lowest concentration of SOMA that can still work efficiently. For clinical trials, the inhaler company will also prepare for us placebo inhalers that will contain powdered lactose sugar instead of SOMA.

As soon as the various dose inhalers were delivered, the scientists tried them on themselves and agreed that the lowest efficacious concentration that still worked well was 0.01 milligram per whiff. Thus the scientists learned that a very small amount of SOMA works effectively leading to prices that would not be exorbitant.

Next, the scientists performed drug-stability studies with 0.01 milligram inhalers that had been placed in incubators set to +40, or +50 or +60 degrees centigrade. These inhalers were tested for residual efficacy at one month intervals, both by self inhalation by the team and also by various peptide analysis methods. By using a certain pharmaceutical extrapolative calculation from the above high temperature studies, the scientists found that the SOMA had an expiry date of 2 years (i.e., it is stable for 2 years) when stored at temperatures up to 45°C.

11

Year 2013

After the finish of the stability studies, John said: "The die is cast! Or, being a Latin scholar, I might say "Alea Iacta Est!" . . . Now the time has come to test the SOMA on patients. Sometime ago I have told you that I will be busy writing an IND application. A month ago I finished writing it and immediately submitted it to FDA. FDA has one month to study any application, to deny it, to accept it, or to demand more data. If they did not say anything, it means that they are granting permission to start human clinical trials. The 30th day came and passed yesterday without any contesting letter from FDA! I did not want to bother you with this matter until now, but I can tell you that yesterday a huge burden came off my chest.

As I have already told you, we will conduct limited scale clinical trials in patients. We already know from our own trial as volunteers that the SOMA can cause happiness, euphoria and serenity and now we will test whether it can also cure various mental disorders. For this, we will choose suitable hospital wards or institutions and will ask their directors to perform such clinical trials with us. Most institutions and physicians are very interested in performing clinical trials since they will get financial support for their own research projects from the sponsors of the drug and can also publish papers on the outcome of the clinical trial, if it is successful.

The patients who will agree to take part in any trial (or their family if they are not mentally competent) will have to sign an "informed consent form" before the start. This form is a legally-defined form which lists for the patients all the key facts involved in the clinical trial. It includes trial details such as its purpose, duration, required trial procedures, risks and potential benefits. The "Informed consent form" is not a binding contract, since the patients can withdraw from the trial at any moment without penalty. The patients are also told that half of them (chosen at random) will receive the tested drug and the other half will receive a placebo. In case of a successful drug, the placebo-treated patients will also receive the drug at the end of the trial, free of charge."

When John finished his discourse, Debbie said: "John, when I had taken a statistics course I was told that any survey, and in our case a clinical trial, should take into account as many variables as possible such as gender, race, age, type of population, economic status and so on. How is this going to be reflected In our upcoming clinical trials?"

John said: "Dear Debbie, you have raised a very pertinent and important question! Some years ago I read an interesting study by several scientists whose names escape me now. They reviewed the best available clinical studies of psychiatric drugs for Depression, Bipolar Disorder, Schizophrenia and Attention Deficit Disorder that had involved something like 10,000 patients over several years, they found that not even one Native American was included in the studies and that only two or three of the patients were Hispanic. Of about 3000 schizophrenia patients tested, only three were Asian. Also, among about 1000 patients with bipolar disorder (manic depressive disorder) there were no Hispanics or Asians. Blacks were better represented, but even their numbers in any one study were too small to tell the clinicians anything meaningful. Scientists have generally played down the role of cultural, ethnic and racial factors in the diagnosis, treatment and outcome of mental disorders. This is because modern psychiatry is based on the idea that mental illnesses are primarily organic disorders of the brain. This approach suggests that the symptoms, course, and treatment of disorders ought to be the same whether the patients are from the Caribbean, Canada or Cambodia.

Major mental disorders like Schizophrenia, Bipolar Disorder, Depression, etc. are found worldwide across all racial and ethnic groups. Based on available evidence, the prevalence of mental disorders for racial and ethnic minorities in the United States is similar to that for whites. Therefore, my dear Debbie, and also because of the small number of the patients that we will study in each trial, by necessity we will ignore the effects of gender, age, ethnicity and economic status."

John decided that the first limited clinical trial that they will perform will be carried out with Anorexia nervosa patients and said: "As you know, Anorexia nervosa is an extremely serious eating disorder expressed by a paralyzing fear of getting fat. The patients, mostly ten to eighteen years old girls, live under a regimen of self-imposed starvation in order to lose weight. In more advanced stages of the disorder the patients may even feel a loathing of food and cannot eat even if they wanted to. This disorder causes terrible results—the extreme fasting causes a complete disruption and destruction of all body systems. The body temperature declines, the pulse slows down and the body's resistance against infection disappears. Finally, very serious heart problems develop that cause death. About 5% of all anorectic patients die within several years.

Researchers believe that the reasons for anorexia nervosa are a combination of psychological, biological and socio-cultural pressures at the start of puberty: according to a psychoanalytical approach, the patients (most of them are girls) do not want to mature and therefore fast in order to postpone as much as possible their sexual maturation (indeed, their breasts do not develop and their menstruation cycle either does not appear at all, or disappears). According to other theories, the disorder is due to problematic family ties, especially with the mothers. The girls feel that the only way left to them for independence and control of their fates and bodies is self starvation.

Other theories stress the importance of peer pressure: the need to be thin and beautiful. Ever since the successful model Twiggy, girls today, even very young ones, still believe that they need to be super-skinny in order to be sexy.

There is also a genetic approach to unraveling the cause of anorexia. Geneticists believe that anorectics are prey to a genetic pre-disposition to various emotional disorders such as distress, self hatred, anxiety and depression. Studies have showed that 40% of all anorectics suffer from medium to major depression. It is this finding that prompted me to try our SOMA on anorectics."

All of John's team expressed their approval for the performance of the proposed study and Debbie also said that she met a couple of anorectic girls in the past and agreed that were in a sorry mess.

In order to perform the trial, John approached one of his colleagues, Professor Enid LeBlanc, who was the director of the psychiatric ward in the Massachusetts General Hospital in Boston and also lectured on clinical psychology at Harvard's Medical and graduate schools.

John described the team's personal experiences as volunteer users of the SOMA to Professor LeBlanc and also said that they have received an IND approval from FDA to perform human trials. Professor LeBlanc willingly agreed to carry out a clinical trial with the anorectic patients in her psychiatric ward. She also said that she had waited long for a suitable drug for the treatment of this affliction, adding that the anorectics, at present, take SSRI drugs (mainly Prozac) but with only indifferent results.

Professor LeBlanc recruited 16 anorectic girls by promising them that throughout the 6-week trial they will not be fed forcefully either by a feeding tube or by infusion to the vein. But, she also told them that they will have to attend all meals and that their eating will be supervised by the nurses, as before. The study was a double blind one: only John and his team knew what each coded SOMA inhaler contained. The ward's nurses supervised the daily inhalation process and the trial patients were weighed once a week and their mental state was also evaluated once a week by a questionnaire called the Beck Depression Inventory (BDI) in order to test if there was any improvement in their depressive state. The BDI questionnaire, developed by Dr. Aaron T. Beck, is used to evaluate of the depressive status, since there are no chemical blood tests for determining the severity of depression. The BDI is A 21-question, multiple-choice, self-report inventory that is filled by the patients themselves, is designed for individuals aged 13 and over and is composed of items relating to symptoms of depression such as hopelessness and irritability, cognitions such as guilt, or feelings of being punished, physical symptoms such as fatigue, weight gain or loss and interest in sex. When the test is scored, a value of 0 to 3 is assigned for each answer and the total score obtained assesses the existence and severity of the depression. The standard cut-offs in the BDI are as follows: A score of 0-13: minimal depression; 14–19: mild depression; 20–28: moderate depression, and 29–63: severe depression.

John said: "Dear coleagues, since the BDI is pivotal to our future work, let us take the test ourselves. I will bet that our scores will be very low. Just note that the questions in sections 16 and 18 ("Changes in Sleeping Pattern" and "Changes in Appetite") should produce only one score." John distributed copies of the inventory that Enid gave him and he and his team filled them. True to his prediction, all of them had a very low score.

Beck Depression Inventory (BDI, for self administration):

Symptom	depression symptom	Self Grading
1. Sadness	0 I do not feel sad	
	1 I feel sad much of the time	
	2 I am sad all the time	
	3 I am so sad or unhappy that I cannot stand it	———————
2 Pessimism	0 I am not discouraged about my future	
	1 I feel more discouraged about my future than I used to be	
	2 I do not expect things to work for me	
	3 I feel my future is helpless and will only get worse	———————
3. Past Failure	0 I do not feel like a failure	
	1. I have failed more than I should have	
	2 As I look back I see a lot of failures	
	3 I feel I am a total failure as a person	———————

Symptom	depression symptom	Self Grading
4. loss of Pleasure	0 I get as much pleasure as ever I did from things I enjoy	
	1 I don't enjoy things as much as I used to	
	2 I get very little pleasure from the things I used to enjoy	
	3 I can't get any pleasure from the things I used to enjoy	————
5.Guilty Feeling	0 I don't feel particularly guilty	
	1 I feel guilty over many things that I have done or should have done	
	2 I feel quite guilty most of the time	
	3 I feel guilty all the time	————
6. Punishment Feeling	0 I don't feel I am being punished	
	1 I feel that I may be punished	
	2 I expect to be punished	————
	3 I feel I am being punished	
7. Self-Dislike	0 I feel the same about myself as ever	
	1 I have lost confidence in myself	
	2 I am disappointed in myself	————
	3 I dislike myself	
8. Self Criticalness	0 I don't criticize or blame myself more than usual	
	1 I am more critical of myself than I used to be	
	2 I criticize myself for all my faults	
	3 I blame myself for everything bad that happened	————

Symptom	depression symptom	Self Grading
9. Suicidal thoughts or wishes	0 I don't have any thoughts of killing myself	
	1 I have thoughts of killing myself . But I would not carry them out	
	2 I would like to kill myself	_____
	3 I would kill myself if I had a chance	
10. Crying	0 I don't cry anymore than I used to	
	1 I cry more than I used to	
	2 I cry over every little thing	
	3 I feel like crying, but I can't	_____
11. Agitation	0 I am no more restless or wound-up than usual	
	1 I feel more restless or wound-up than usual	
	2 I am so restless and agitated that it is hard to stay still	
	3 I am so restless or agitated that I have to keep moving or doing something	_____
12. Loss of Interest	0 I have not lost interest in other people or activities	
	1 I am less interested in other people or things than before	
	2 I have lost most of my interests in other people or things	
	3 It is hard to get interested in anything	_____

Symptom	depression symptom	Self Grading
13. Indecisiveness	0 I make decisions about as well as ever	
	1 I find it more difficult to make decisions than usual	
	2 I have much greater difficulty in making decisions than I used to	
	3 I have trouble making any decisions	_____
14. Worthlessness	0 I do not feel I am worthless	
	1 I do not consider myself as worthwhile and useful as I used to	
	2 I feel more worthless as compared to other people	_____
	3 I feel utterly worthless	
15. Loss of Energy	0 I have as much energy as ever	
	1 I have less energy than I used to have	
	2 I don't have enough energy to do very much	
	3 I don't have enough energy to do anything	_____

Symptom	depression symptom	Self Grading
16. Changes in Sleeping Pattern	0 I have not experienced any change in my sleeping patern	
	1a I sleep somewhat more than usual 1b I sleep somewhat less than usual	
	2a I sleep a lot more than usual 2b I sleep a lot less than usual	
	3a I sleep most of the day 3b I wake up 1-2 hours early and can't go back to sleep	_____
17. Irritability	0 I am no more irritable than usual	
	1 I am more irritable than usual	
	2 I am much more irritable than usual	
	3 I am irritable all the time	_____
18. Changes in Appetite	0 I have not experienced any change in my appetite	
	1a My appetite is somewhat less than usual 1b My appetite is somewhat greater than usual	
	2a My appetite is much less than before 2b My appetite is much greater than usual	
	3a I have no appetite at all 3b I crave food all the time	_____

Symptom	depression symptom	Self Grading
19. concentration difficulty	0 I can concentrate as well as ever	
	1 I can't concentrate as well as usual	
	2 It is hard to keep my mind on anything for very long	
	3 I find I can't concentrate on anything	_____
20. Tiredness or Fatigue	0 I am no more tired or fatigued than usual	
	1 I get more tired and fatigued more easily than usual	
	2 I am too tired or fatigued to do a lot of things that I used to do	
	3 I am too tired or fatigued to do most of the things I used to do	_____
21. Loss of Interest in Sex	0 I have not noticed any recent change in my interest in sex	
	1 I am less interested in sex than I used to be	
	2 I am much less interested in sex now	_____
	3 I have lost interest in sex completely	

The experiment with the anorectic girls started and their end-of-weeks' weights and Beck's scores were recorded. The weight-increases and the BDI results that were obtained by the end of the clinical trial relative to the start, were summarized in a table:

Summary of the results of the 6-week trial in anorectic girls

patient No.	Increase in weight (kg)	Change in Beck's Score*
1	2.9	+3
2	7.9	-15
3	8.7	-22
4	2.1	+3
5	8.0	-25
6	2.1	+4
7	8.4	-25
8	2.2	+3
9	9.0	-22
10	8.5	-14
11	2.6	+4
12	1.2	+3
13	7.6	-20
14	2.4	+5
15	7.7	-15
16	2.0	+5

*) Note: A minus sign in the Beck's score means a reduction in the degree of depression

After the opening of the code, the mean results were calculated for the 8 SOMA and the 8 Placebo patients. These mean results are presented in the next table:

Means of weight-gains and chage in Beck's scores for SOMA and Plcebo patients

Type of treatment	mean change in weight (Kg)	Mean change in Beck's score
SOMA	+8.2	-19.7
Placebo	+2.2	+3.8

The results of the tables indicated very clearly that the SOMA patients exhibited great improvements in mood and nice increases in weights. The joyful parents of the improved girls calmored to know the identity of their benefactors, made visits to the lab, and inundated the team with flowers and chocolates. Learning from this experience, the team decided to demand anonimity from the staffs that will perform their clinical trials in the future.

At John's request, Professor LeBlanc prepared a detailed report of the results which was to be presented eventually to pharmaceutical companies. She also wrote a scientific paper on the results which also bore the four scientists' names, but she was forced to wait for John's green light for its submission to a journal.

Professor LeBlanc asked the team for additional inhalers for all her other anorectic patients, but John was forced to refuse saying that by FDA laws he is unable to fulfil her wish. On hearing his answer she sighed, knowing that she has to continue to try to save the lives of her anorectic patients with conventional feeding methods and with SSRIs. To "console" her John said: "dear Enid, I was very happy with your excellent handling of our trial and I plan to carry additional clinical trials with you for more disorders if you would agree." And being in an expansive and elated mood because of their success in their first trial, he recited the memorable lines of the poem that was written by Emma Lazarus in 1883 and is inscribed inside the Statue of Liberty:

"Give me your tired, your poor, your huddled masses yearning

to breathe free, the wretched refuse of your teeming shore.

Send these, the homeless, tempest-tossed to me,

I lift my lamp beside the golden door!"

Both Enid and John smiled, shook hands on their "contract" and went their ways.

12

Year 2013

Several days after the anorectics' trial, John decided to perform a trial with elderly frail inmates in a nursing home and addressed his colleagues: "dear friends, let me cut you in on a secret – we humans are not immortal. True, we are not as ephemeral as butterflies and flies whose life span is 2-25 days. But still, our life-spans are measured in several scores of years, barring wars, accidents and disease."

Hearing this profound revelation, Ben opened his eyes in fright and said in a whining voice: "Wow, no one has ever told me this secret before. Had I known it, I would have refused to be born" . . . Then he added: "But seriously now, my parents told me that at the age of five I came to them crying saying that I don't want to die. They had a hard time consoling me" . . .

John waited patiently for Ben to finish and continued: "Luckily for us, it is a blessed characteristic of human nature that we generally manage to suppress this unsavory fact. However, this kind of defense mechanism does not work anymore for the elderly. Therefore, while we were still progressing with our anorectics' trial, I had already decided to test whether the SOMA will be able to alleviate the sad psychological plight and depression of elderly frail and mentally frail persons. I made arrangements to carry out a trial among elderly frail persons sheltered in a nursing home in Boston which is called the "Amity nursing home." This nursing home treats very low income elderly and mentally frail persons and is supported mainly by contributions. The medical care in the nursing home is given by two internists and three psychiatrists and is headed by one of the psychiatrists, Dr. Robert Benchly, that I met in a psychological convention in Boston two years ago.

Who are defined as "elderly frail and mentally frail persons"? The elderly frail are men and women who are generally dependent on others for the activities of daily life and are often in institutional care. Generally they are not mobile by themselves and often require regular drug therapy. Mentally frail persons are those who suffer from one of many possible mental disorders. As a rule, elderly persons are at high risk for mental disorders with most studies citing an incidence rate of about 30%. Among their debilitating mental illnesses one finds depression, at 35% prevalence, and cognitive disturbances of dementing disorders such as Alzheimer's disease, anxiety states, phobic behavior and delirium.

John added that after describing their successful results with the anorectics, Dr. Benchly was very eager to carry out a SOMA trial. John asked him to enlist in the upcoming trial only elderly frail persons that suffer from depression, and not mentally frail ones. Dr. Benchly said that at present he treats his depressed elderly patients with SSRI or with anti-psychotic drugs and would gladly like to add another good anti-depressant drug to his arsenal.

The trial was planned to be a coded, double-blind one, in which the physicians and nurses would not know what every enrolled inmate would receive. The Amity staff obtained informed consents from 48 inmates (20 men and 28 women) after promising them that the drug has no side-effects and that at the end of the 6 months' trial, if the drug would work as expected, the placebo patients would also receive the real drug. For the test, the SOMA group patients received a SOMA inhaler and placebo pills, whereas the placebo patients received placebo inhalers and their regular real anti-depressant drugs.

One of the parameters tested in the trial, aside from recording the depressive state of the inmates with the BDI questionnaire and the amount of food they ingested (depressed inmates may refuse to eat, or will eat only very sparingly), was to follow their mortality statistics. The mortality rate of elderly frail inmates in nursing homes is notoriously high. They die of depression, "broken heart" and ill health. Some of the depressed elderly inmates manage to commit suicide, in spite of the staff's close watch.

John's team attached great importance to the results of the trial, reasoning that the inmates represented a "worst case" situation for depression. They knew that if they would succeed in combating the depression of the elderly, the sky is the limit for the SOMA. Soon after the start of the trial, the scientists and the medical and nursing staff were overjoyed to see that about half of the patients exhibited great improvement in mood, exhibiting tranquility and even euphoria. When the "blinding" code was opened at the end of the six months trial, the staff could confirm that those inmates who were cured of their depression were SOMA takers. Moreover, the survival rate of the SOMA group was about three fold higher that of the Placebo group! Dr. Benchly and his medical staff were very vocal in their praises and wrote an extensive formal enthusiastic report of the trial's results for John and his team. Like Professor LeBlank, Dr. Benchly wrote a scientific paper on the results to be published after FDA's certification of the SOMA.

13

Year 2013

In the aftermath of the successful clinical trial with the elderly frail persons, John decided to perform a clinical trial with patients of Major Depressive Disorder. John considered this target to be the most appropriate one for the SOMA and Ben, remembering his depressed friend from Philadelphia, as well as Debbie and Lucia, whole-heartedly agreed with him.

John said: "after the successful culmination of the anorexia trial I promised Enid that we would perform additional clinical trials with her. Two weeks ago I called her and suggested a trial with her major depression patients. Let me tell you that her shout of joy on the phone caused me to lose the hearing in my right ear for a few seconds . . . As a result, she had been recruiting, and told me yesterday that all her major depression patients from the outpatient clinic agreed to participate in the trial.

When we go to meet Enid, I already want you to know some facts about this very serious affliction and its presumed causes. Ben is already familiar with the subject, but you, my lovely Debbie and my faithful Lucia, hark to my discourse:

"The words of Stephen Foster in his song "Old folks at home" ("Way down Upon the Swanee River") quite aptly describe the state of many depressive patients:

"All de world am sad and dreary,

Ebry where I roam . . ."

Major depressive disorder, also known as recurrent depressive disorder, clinical depression, major depression, unipolar depression, or unipolar disorder, is a mental disorder characterized by an all-encompassing low mood accompanied by low self-esteem, and by a loss of interest or pleasure in normally enjoyable activities. It is an extremely debilitating condition which adversely affects a person's family, his work or school life, sleeping and eating habits and general health. Depressed people may be preoccupied with, or ruminate over, thoughts and feelings of worthlessness, inappropriate guilt or regret, helplessness, hopelessness and self-hatred. In severe cases, depressed people may have symptoms of psychosis which include delusions or, less commonly, unpleasant hallucinations. Other symptoms of depression include poor concentration and memory, withdrawal from social situations and activities, reduced sex drive and thoughts of death or suicide. Insomnia is also common, and the patients have shorter life expectancies than those without depression, in part because of greater susceptibility to physical illnesses and suicide. About

3.4% of people with major depression in the United States commit suicide, or, put another way—up to 60% of people who committed suicide had major depression or another mood disorder.

The most common onset time of major depression is between the ages of 20 and 30 years, with a later peak between 30 and 40 years. Diagnosis is based on the patient's self-reported experiences, his behavior as described by relatives or friends, and a mental status examination such as the Beck Depression Inventory.

Typically, patients are treated with tricyclic antidepressants and anti-psychotic drugs and in many cases also receive psychotherapy. Hospitalization may be necessary in cases with associated self-neglect or a significant risk of harm to self or others.

A minority of major depression cases are treated with electroconvulsive therapy (ECT) under general anesthesia. Most recently, major depression is also treated by a technique known as Repetitive transcranial magnetic stimulation (rTMS) in which a powerful magnetic field is used to stimulate the brain. This therapy does not require anesthesia as with ECT and does not cause any confusion or memory loss such as those encountered with ECT. Both rTMS and ECT treatments are efficient, but require up 20 sessions to obtain good results and therefore cannot be used widely as will, hopefully, our SOMA."

Forearmed with the information concerning major depression that John fed them, the scientists met Enid who told them that she recruited 72 ambulatory patients that make regular weekly visits to her out-patient clinic.

The trial was again a double blind one. The patients were distributed into 2 groups with about an equal distribution of ages and gender. The trial was slated to last for 4 weeks. The placebo inhaler patients received their regular drugs, while the SOMA inhaler patients were given placebo pills that looked and tasted just like their previous regular drugs. They were asked to report every week to the out-patient clinic and to describe their mental condition.

One week after the start of the trial, Enid called John and his team and happily informed them that about half of the patients reported a feeling of great serenity and happiness which was also reflected in their faces. Instead of looking ashen and miserable, their lines of misery completely disappeared. The opening of the code at the end of the four-week trial completely vindicated Enid's empirical observations.

John told his team that he plans to offer the major depression indication as the one which will be tested in future big clinical trials intended to obtain certification by the FDA.

14

Year 2013

A few days after the completion of the trial with the elderly frail and major depression patients, John and Debbie came early to the lab and saw that its normally locked door was ajar. On entering they saw that the lab was in complete mess: bottles with chemicals lay broken, the refrigerators and freezers were open and glass tubes and containers lay broken on the floor. The two big safes that John bought for storage of SOMA inhalers remained closed, but bore the signs of break-in efforts. John called the campus police who questioned the building's security guards. Investigation revealed that a man wearing work coveralls and carrying a toolbox enetered last evening saying that he was called for an emergency repair of an instrument in Professor Novick's lab. Since the man knew John's name, the guard, new to the job, let him in without asking for credentials. This "technician" left after 10 PM. John came to the obvious conclusion that one of the anorectic girls of the SOMA trial or her parents, told their friends about the new "wonder drug" and the names of the scientists who invented it . . . John immediately asked the campus maintenance unit to install a strong break-safe door at the entrance to the lab at his grant's expense, and to put steel grilles on the windows.

The whole team worked hard all day to put the lab back in order and to obtain new chemicals and materials to replace the spilled ones. Tired after their hard work, John and Debbie went to bed. John, who suffered occasionally from insomnia, went over the day's events and finally was ready to "count sheep." Suddenly he sat in bed, grabbed his head and moaned softly, in order not to wake Debbie.

"Woe is me! He thought. "What shall we do? We have created a monster – an extremely dangerous drug that is worse than all street drugs combined! We will never be able to market it. Within a short time, news of the non-addictive euphoria-inducing-drug will spread all over the world. As a result, all SOMA producing plants and all drugstores will be plundered by criminals for selling the SOMA in the streets. Even the biggest imaginable pharmaceutical factories in the world will not be able to produce enough SOMA inhalers to satisfy the needs of the billions of inhabitants of the world. This will lead to the eruption of drug wars world-wide!

Thus John lay awake all night in agony. He decided not to wake Debbie in order to save her a few hours of sorrow.

Next day, John came bleary-eyed and withered to the lab. Debbie already saw his state early morning and pressed him to tell her what was wrong. In an anguished voice he told her of his gloomy prediction and she sadly agreed that he was right, but gamely tried to console him. When Ben and Lucia arrived, John told them of his fears and apprehensions. They sobered up when he described the scenario as he envisioned it last night, and sadly admitted that he was right.

At the end of the gloomy discussion, Ben went to his office, planning to call Moira and to tell her of the unfortunate ruin of the SOMA's prospects. suddenly he froze in his chair and started to mull over a glimmer of an idea which became more and more coherent with each passing second! He was sure that his idea could save the SOMA for the world! He hurried to John's office and said: "John, Eureka! I have a tremendous idea that will save our brain-child."

John raised his crestfallen face and extinguished eyes to Ben who said: "Listen my friend! There are several philanthropic billionaires in the US and the world who regularly contribute a part of their fortune to wellfare through foundations that they had established, and their number is steadily growing. Among them are the "heavy" and well-known billionaires Bill Kelly and Warren Brooks. Bill Kelly established the Bill and Jeanne Kelly foundation to which both Kelly and Brooks contributed very large sums of money. The foundation's aim is to increase healthcare and education and help poor people in the world. We will approach Kelly and Brooks first, describe our results, show them Professor LeBlanc's and Dr. Benchly's summary reports and the IND granting by the FDA. In addition, we will let them try the SOMA for themselves so that they will understand how important it is going to be for all humanity. I am quite sure that we can persuade them, or some other philanthropic billionaires, to help us certify the drug and to build huge factories all over the world in order to produce secretly billions of SOMA inhalers. Only after we would accumulate the necessary large number of inhalers for all humanity several times over we will publicise our invention and distribute the SOMA to all humanity, free of charge!"

John opened his eyes in wonder and the color came back to his face. He stood up, hugged Ben and they went happily together to the lab. John, pointing to Ben, said: "Look at this guy and praise him among all nations and extole his virtues for all to hear! He is the MAN, our hero! He found an excellent way to save the SOMA!" Ben then described his ideas to the girls, who applauded him enthusiastically.

Debbie said: "What a great idea, I am sure that it will work. But, in the meantime, how can we block leaks about the SOMA from the participants of our future clinical trials?"

Riding on the wave of the creative imagination that he had already displayed, Ben said: "First, we will ask the medical staffs of our next trials not to divulge our identity. Secondly, the medical staffs will warn all the tested patients that the drug will only work on them alone, since it will correct a defective gene that they carry and that caused their disorder. They will also tell the patients not share their inhalers with family or friends, because healthy people lack the defective gene and, as a result, even one whiff of the SOMA will damage their brains! The patients will be told also that they will receive one inhaler with 31 daily doses per month and that if they share their inhalers with family or friends, they will miss doses at the end of the month, and will suffer very painful withdrawal symptoms."

The rest of the day went on joyfully since the scientists knew that they had averted an unforseen huge disaster and that, thanks to John's and Ben's acumen, they had just barely missed setting the world on fire!

John said: "As I have already told you in the past, each new drug must undergo rigorous clinical testing in many patients before it is approved by health authorities. The performance of such testing requires a great deal of effort and large sums of money. Therefore, In addition to the hiring of a company for the large-scale production of SOMA inhalers for us, we will ask Kelly and Brooks (or any other philanthropists that will agree to help) to contract the services of a large CRO company. Such a company specializes in the performance of clinical trials for sponsors of new drugs. It recruits patients, medical centers, physicians, nurses and pharmacists, maintains a medical file for each patient, performs the statistical analyses of the results of the trials and prepares the extensive paperwork required by FDA prior for the approval of a drug. Meanwhile, we will continue our imited clinical trials in order to determine which additional disorders the SOMA can, hopefully, cure.

15

Year 2013

Following their success in the clinical trials with the anorectic patients, the elderly frail persons and the major depression patients, the scientists started a clinical trial with Schizophrenic patients. True to John's promise to Professor Leblanc, the trial was to be carried out again at her outpatient clinic. Before planning the trial, John and his team turned to the Internet sites of the National Institute of Mental Health in order to learn more about the disorder. This is what they read:

"Schizophrenia is a mental disorder typified by disintegration of the process of thinking and of emotional responsiveness. It is most commonly manifested by auditory hallucinations, paranoid or bizarre delusions, disorganized thinking and is accompanied by significant social or occupational dysfunctions. The onset of symptoms typically occurs in young adulthood, with a global lifetime prevalence of around 1.5%. Diagnosis is based on the patient's self-reported experiences and observed behavior.

The development of Schizophrenia in patients is ascribed to 3 factors:

1) A pathologic factor – a problem in the development of the embryo's brain, or degeneration of the brain's neurons after their development.

2) A genetic factor – when one of the parents is schizophrenic, the frequency of schizophrenia in his offspring goes up to 10% and when both parents have schizophrenia, the frequency of the disorder goes up to 40%. When one sibling of identical twins is sick, the other one has a 50% chance of becoming schizophrenic. Still, schizophrenia is, apparently, not linearly inherited; otherwise, the occurrence in both siblings should have been 100%.

3) Schizophrenics have an overactive dopamine system that acts in the mesolimbic pathway of the brain. Therefore, Dopamine antagonists can help regulate this system by "turning down" Dopamine activity and are helpful in some of the patients.

Despite the etymology of the term—from the Greek roots: skhizein "to split" and phrēn "mind"—schizophrenia is not a "split mind" disorder. The "real" split mind disorder is called "Dissociative Identity Disorder (DID)", which is also known as "multiple personality disorder" or "split personality." People often mistakenly confuse schizophrenia with DID.

In more serious cases of schizophrenia—where there is risk to the patient himself and to others—involuntary hospitalization may be necessary. Schizophrenia is thought, mainly, to affect cognition, but it also contributes to chronic problems with emotion and behavior, major depression and anxiety disorders. The lifetime occurrence of drug abuse in schizophrenic patients is around 40%. Social problems such as long-term unemployment and poverty are common. As a result, the prevalence of Schizophrenia is very high among untreated homeless people—around 10-20%. The average life expectancy of people with this disorder is 10 to 12 years shorter than of those without it, due to increased prevalence of physical health problems and a high suicide rate (about 5%).

As already described above, schizophrenic patients may experience hallucinations (most commonly hearing voices), delusions (often bizarre or persecutory in nature) and disorganized thinking and speech. The latter may range from a loss of train of thought, to sentences that are only loosely connected in meaning, up to an incoherent speech known as "word salad." There is often an observable pattern of emotional difficulty, such as lack of responsiveness or motivation. As a result of impairment in social cognition, the patients exhibit symptoms of paranoia and social isolation. In one subtype, the person may be largely mute, remain motionless in bizarre postures, or exhibit purposeless agitation. The peak years for the onset of schizophrenia are late adolescence and early adulthood.

Schizophrenia is described in terms of positive and negative (or deficit) symptoms. The term positive symptoms refers to symptoms that are present in schizophrenics and not in healthy people. These include delusions, auditory hallucinations and thought disorders. Negative symptoms refer to behaviors exhibited by healthy persons, but are absent in schizophrenic ones. Common positive symptoms include flat or blunted emotions, poverty of speech, inability to experience pleasure, lack of desire to form relationships and lack of motivation. Research suggests that negative symptoms contribute more to poor quality of life, functional disability and the burden on others, than do positive ones.

Several years ago the plight of schizophrenic patients came to the attention of the general public in a touching movie "A Beautiful Mind" that described the life of John Forbes Nash who won the Nobel Prize in Economic Sciences in 1994.

As already described above, schizophrenics exhibit unusually high dopamine activity in the mesolimbic pathway of the brain. The mainstay of treatments of schizophrenia are antipsychotic drugs such as Clozapine, Risperdal or Zyprexa. These drugs block Dopamine receptors, prevent their activity and can induce complete recovery in up to 20% of the patients, whilst in others they are only partially effective. However, the side-effects of these anti-psychotic drugs are very significant: inability to start moving, or inability to stand still, involuntary spasm in the face, throat, eyes, tongue or chin, marked increase in weight and loss of libido. As a result, many patients refuse to take them. Recently, however, anti schizophrenia drugs such as Risperdal and others are administered as depot medications by injection. These drug depots allow a slow release of drug throughout 2-4 weeks and cause lighter side-effects. At present, however, these depot drugs are very expensive.

Schizophrenia is a terrible affliction for life, and Enid and John's team hoped to cure the patients, or at least to alleviate their symptoms without the bad side-effects encountered with antipsychotic drugs. Their hope for cure or improvement was based on John's finding of the new "Endorphin to Serotonin pathway". Since Endorphin decreases the synthesis of Dopamine and increases that of Serotonin, they hoped that the SOMA will have a good chance of helping the schizophrenics.

As in all the team's clinical trials till now, the trial with the schizophrenic patients was a double-blind one. It included 64 men and women of which half of them received SOMA inhalers plus a placebo pill that looked exactly like their usual anti-psychotic drug, while the other half received placebo inhalers and their regular drug.

Success in the trial was immediately apparent and unequivocal. The condition of about half of the patients improved markedly after 2-4 days from the start of the trial, regardless of whether they suffered from positive or negative symptoms. Therefore, the double-blind code was eagerly broken much earlier than planned and confirmed that the marvelously cured patients were indeed those treated with SOMA inhalers.

As a result of their victory over one of the worst mental disorders, John decided to offer the schizophrenia indication for testing by "their" future CRO company (in addition to the Major Depression indication).

16

Year 2013

After the successful termination of the schizophrenia trial, John addressed his team: "Dear colleagues, so far we have been very successful in proving the efficacy of SOMA in several mental disorders; but, "eating whets the appetite." Therefore, with a certain degree of justified Hubris, I am greedy for more successes. Before, as an experimental neuropharmacologist and a teacher, I knew a lot about mental disorders in theoretical terms but I was mostly interested in fighting depression. But now, when confronted face to face with the poor patients that we encountered in Enid's psychiatric ward, I am keen to cure all mental disorders, no less" . . . John's Colleagues nodded their heads in agreement.

John and his team met Enid again and she said: "Dear marvelous colleagues, you have come to us like Manna from heaven and like spring water in the desert! Before you came, my staff and I stumbled along sadly with only middling success. Now, all that has changed!

Therefore, God and the SOMA willing, let us try to cure Bi-polar disorder. This disorder, which is also known as manic-depressive disorder, is a very serious mental illness that causes sudden shifts in a person's mood, energy and ability to function. The disorder was termed "Bipolar", because its patients shift from a pole of Mania—an overly joyful and overexcited state—to a pole of Depression and back again. These shifts in mood are quite different from the normal ups-and-downs that everyone encounters through life. The symptoms of bipolar disorder are extremely severe. Many famous leaders, musicians, writers and artists were identified as suffering from the disorder, either by their historically-documented behavior, or by their own public disclosures. Let me mention just a few of many names: Vincent Van-Gogh, Jackson Pollock, Theodore Roosevelt, Virginia Wolfe, Edgar Allen Poe, Abraham Lincoln, Johann Wolfgang von Goethe, Napoleon Bonaparte, Charles Dickens, Winston Churchill, Robert Schumann, Ludwig van Beethoven, Jack London, Charles Dickens, William Faulkner, Ernest Hemingway, Mark Twain, Rosemary Clooney, Florence Nightingale, Lord Byron, Alfred Lord Tennyson, Hermann Hesse, John Keats, Sylvia Plath, Hans Christian Andersen, Vivian Leigh, Stephen Fry and Kurt Cobain. Of this very limited list alone three persons had committed suicide: Hemmingway, Plath and Cobain.

The symptoms of the manic episode of the disorder are as follows:

In mania, the patients exhibit a long period of feeling "high"—an overly happy or outgoing mood, but they are also irritable, feeling agitated, "jumpy" or "wired-up." During this episode, the patients talk at a very fast rate, jump from one idea to another, their thoughts are constantly racing, they are easily distracted and start new projects without much thought. In addition, they need only little sleep and exhibit an unrealistic belief in their abilities. As a result, they take part in a lot of pleasurable high-risk behaviors such as spending sprees, impulsive sex and risky business investments.

Patients with bipolar disorder also experience episodes of hypomania. During hypomanic episodes, the patient may have increased energy and creativity levels but these are not as severe as in typical mania and do not require emergency care. Patient in a hypomanic episode feels very well, are highly productive and functions well. They may not even feel that anything is wrong with them and only their family and friends can recognize their hypomanic symptoms. The hypomanic state does not last long and eventually converts into a manic or a depressive state.

Sometimes, a person with severe episodes of mania or depression may also experience psychotic symptoms such as hallucinations or delusions. As a result, such patients are sometimes wrongly diagnosed as having schizophrenia.

The symptoms of a depressive episode include the following: a long period of feeling worried or empty, a loss of all interest in activities once enjoyed (including sex), feeling tired or "slowed down", having problems concentrating, remembering and making decisions, being restless, sad or irritable, changing eating—sleeping—or other habits, thinking of death or suicide, or actually even attempting it.

Bipolar disorder is commonly treated with mood stabilizers such as Lithium and Valproic acid. Sometimes, antipsychotic—and antidepressant drugs are also used, along with the mood stabilizer. In general, patients continue treatment with mood stabilizers for years. But, as is the case with schizophrenia, many patients stop taking their drugs because of their very serious side-effects:

1) Lithium's side-effects include loss of coordination, excessive thirst, frequent urination, blackouts, seizures, slurred speech, fast or slow or irregular or pounding heartbeat, hallucinations, changes in vision, itching, rash, swelling of the eyes, face, lips, tongue, throat, hands, feet, ankles, or lower part of the legs.

2) Valproic acid's side-effects are changes in weight, nausea, stomach pain, vomiting, anorexia and loss of appetite. This drug can also cause damage to the liver or the pancreas.

Some of the patients stop taking their drugs for fear that they will stem the pleasure and flow of the creativity that they experience during the hypomanic stage. Therefore, dear saviors," concluded Enid in a way that made us blush, "let us try to help these really miserable people."

Enid enrolled 78 outpatients that were in an active state of mania or depression at the time of the trial. As in the previous trials, one half of the patients, chosen at random, received SOMA inhalers and placebo pills that looked and tasted like their regular drugs and the other half received their regular true drug plus placebo inhalers.

The scientists entered the trial with some trepidation for 2 reasons:

A. Aside from the knowledge that bipolar disorder also has a genetic back-ground, the mechanism of its induction was still obscure.

B. The scientists were sure that the SOMA, because of its already proven efficiency, will help patients in the depression pole, but they were afraid that the SOMA might quickly cause them to switch from depression into a manic stage.

In spite of the team's misgivings, the SOMA worked beautifully! Even before opening the blind code it became obvious that one half of the patients exhibited a complete cure! Enid and her staff were sure that they must belong to the SOMA group since they had never witnessed such miraculous cures before: patients in a manic episode moved from a manic to a hypomanic state in one day and within two additional days started to express the same serenity and bliss expected from a SOMA treatment. The depressive patients in this same half also became happy and serene after one or two days. At Enid's urgent behest and because of John's own impatience, the scientists hastily broke the double-blind code and were relieved and overjoyed to find that all the miraculous cures indeed happened in the SOMA group!

All the trial's patients, whether they were from the SOMA or Placebo groups, received 'take home'

SOMA inhalers for 12 months. They were instructed to report back to the clinic during this period in case of unexplained reversals or unusual bad side-effects. No patient reported back early. As usual, all of the patients were told to prevent their relatives or friends from trying the SOMA, since it is extremely dangerous to "normal" people . . .

17

Year 2013

In one of the meetings that John and his team held with Enid, Debbie said: "Professor LeBlanc, I have heard a lot about patients who suffer from "split personalities" or DID (Dissociative Identity Disorder) and during our Schizophrenia trial I learned from the Internet that this disorder should not be confused with schizophrenia. What, is it then?"

Enid said: "Dear Debbie, you have raised a very interesting and somewhat controversial issue; Dissociative Identity Disorder (DID), which is also termed Multiple Personality Disorder (MPD), describes a condition in which a person displays multiple distinct identities or personalities known as "alter egos" or "alters." Each "alter" has its own pattern of perceiving and interacting with the environment. Some psychiatrists maintain that DID does not actually exist as a valid medical diagnosis, whereas others think that it does exist. A third group maintains that DID exists, but is induced as a side-effect of psychological treatment. I have, at present, three DID women patients that I treat without worrying about the controversy that I just described.

The diagnosis of DID requires that at least two "alters" will routinely take control of the individual's behavior and that each "alter" should not have any memory of the other "alters." These changes in identity, loss of memory and the awaking in unexplained locations and situations, cause a chaotic life. The incidence of DID is extremely low, but had gained exposure in episodes of crime-investigating television series where the culprit faked DID in order to escape punishment. DID patients demonstrate a variety of symptoms with wide fluctuations; their functioning can vary from severe impairment to normal or high abilities. Symptoms can include: attitudes and beliefs that differ across "alters", severe memory loss, depression, flashbacks of abuse/trauma, sudden anger without a justified cause, lack of intimacy and personal connections, frequent panic and anxiety attacks and auditory hallucinations of the "alters" inside their minds.

Different "alter" states may show distinct physiological changes and ElectroEncephaloGraphy (EEG) studies have shown distinct differences between alters in some subjects, while in other patients, the EEG patterns did not show such changes. Brain MRI studies have corroborated the transitions of identity in some DID sufferers. They have shown differing cerebral blood flows in the brain in different "alters" and distinct differences overall between DID patients and a healthy control group. One study in twins suggested that DID might have a genetic background since it was present in both twins.

A high percentage of patients reported child abuse. DID patients often report that they had experienced severe physical and sexual abuse during their childhood. Therefore it was suggested that DID is strongly related to childhood trauma, rather than to an underlying electrophysiological dysfunction. Those psychologists who treat DID as a legitimate disorder, suggest the following mechanisms for its development: the child is harmed by a trusted caregiver (often a parent or guardian) and "splits off" the awareness and memory of the traumatic event in order to be able to survive in the damaging relationship. These "split off" memories and feelings go into the subconscious and are experienced later in the form of a separate personality. If the abuse happened repeatedly at different times, it causes the development of several "alters", each containing different memories and performing different functions. Thus the DID becomes a coping mechanism for the individual when faced with further stressful situations.

However, as I have already mentioned, some investigators believe that the symptoms of DID are inadvertently created by therapists in suggestible patients upon using certain treatment techniques. The skeptics have observed that a small number of therapists are responsible for diagnosing the majority of persons with DID and that these patients did not report sexual abuse or manifested "alters" before treatment had begun, although this fact does really not prove much.

DID does not resolve spontaneously and the severity of the symptoms vary over time. With psychological treatment, patients with DID eventually recover.

As I have already told you, I have at present three women under treatment whose advance under psychotherapy is slow. What do you think John, shall we give them SOMA? The disorder has a very low occurrence rate, but all my patients are dear to me. John aswered: "By all means, Enid. Even if the SOMA will not cure their dissociative state, it may, at the very least, cure their depression."

Enid gave her patients SOMA inhalers for one month and stopped their psychological therapy during this month. A month later, the three women reported back and said that they feel great euphoria and calm and that their relatives have told them that during the last month they have exhibited only one "alter" that conformed to their own "true" original selves. Enid and the womens' therapist tested the women by trying to invoke their other "alters" under hypnosis, but none came to fore.

This success gave Enid another reason to regard John and his team as true "miracle workers" whose remedy is not the "snake oil" of con-men in the nineteenth century, but a real cure-all elixir! She said: "Dear friends, I know that several times I have embarassed you with my 'hero worshiping' attitude . . . But you ought to realize that although I have reached the top of my profession, being a professor heading an important department, there had never been a single day in the past 30 years of my career that I did not rue my decision to specialize in

Psychiatry. Surgeons and physicians in other branches of "physical" Medicine often achieve complete cures that I envy. In my line of work, complete successes and cures are too few. I see much anguish both in the patients and in their relatives, and I feel completely helpless. It is true that there are some useful drugs that treat various mental disorders, but as you know, many patients refuse to take them because of their side-effects. Now I am living through a wonderful period! God bless you—you have made a not so young lady happy!

18

Year 2013

After completing the Bi-polar disorder trial, John and his team turned to tackle a very serious affliction – that of the Post Traumatic Stress Disorder (PTSD). John told his colleagues: "I am especially keen to try to cure PTSD patients, because of a personal reason. I think that I have already told you some time ago that my father suffers from PTSD. He participated in the Vietnam War as a USMC first lieutenant commanding a platoon. For his actions during the war he was highly decorated, receiving a silver star, a bronze star and two Purple Heart medals aside from several citations and various South Vietnamese medals. On release from the army he was treated for PTSD in Boston with only little success. He once told me that he still experiences recurring terrible visions of some of his men being wounded or dying on the battlefield. He also said that he constantly suffers from a "survivor's guilt feeling" of being alive when many of his men died, possibly as a result of faulty combat decisions that he might have made. In addition, he could not understand the disdain that people in the US felt for the Vietnam War combatants who were told upon enlistment that they are going to fight for their country and for democracy. I think that it is shameful that veterans of unpopular conflicts such as the Vietnam War, have been often blamelessly criticized. When we started with the SOMA trials, it had long been my intention to enroll my father as a subject in a PTSD trial."

To perform the trial, John called Enid and found that she and her staff do not treat PTSD patients in their ward or outpatient clinic. She told John to contact PTSD experts in the veterans' Affairs (VA) Healthcare System in Boston. She said that this system consists of a set of hospitals run by the United States Department of Veterans Affairs and offers both physical and mental health treatments in several locations. Of these Bostonian campuses, Enid recommended that they will contact the Winchester campus which has a nationally known PTSD—and drug-abuse program that is managed by a colleague of hers, Dr. William Trent. She said that Dr. Trent's program tries to help men and women veterans develop skills, to maintain drug abstinence, and to manage PTSD symptoms. Enid was sure that Dr. Trent will be very happy to carry out a SOMA trial with them and promised to help with Dr. Trent if need should arise.

As was their habit before starting a trial, Ben, Debbie and Lucia consulted the Internet site of the National Institutes of Mental Health, in order to learn more about the disorder (John was already quite knowledgeable about it). This is what they read: "PTSD is an anxiety disorder that can develop after exposure to a terrifying event or ordeal in which grave physical harm occurred, or was threatened. Traumatic events that may trigger PTSD include violent physical or sexual assaults, domestic violence, natural or human-caused disasters, abuse, accidents, or military combat. PTSD caused by military combat had been termed "shell shock" in past wars.

When in danger, it's natural to feel afraid. This fear triggers many split-second changes in the body that are needed to defend it against the danger or to avoid it – the so called "fight-or-flight" response. In PTSD, this reaction acquires an additional aspect: people who have PTSD may feel stressed or frightened even when they're no longer in danger. Anyone can get PTSD at any age. Moreover, not everyone with PTSD has been through a dangerous event. Some people get PTSD after a friend or family member experienced danger or was harmed. The sudden, unexpected death of a loved one can also cause PTSD.

According to information supplied by the National Institute of Mental Health, about 15% of men and 10% of women among Vietnam veterans were found to suffer from PTSD. Many of them still suffer from terrible nightmares causing them to wake up in shrieks, drenched with cold sweat. In addition, it is estimated that several millions of American adults of the age of 18 and older have or had PTSD after violent personal assaults.

PTSD can cause many symptoms. These symptoms can be grouped into three categories:

1. Re-experiencing symptoms and flashbacks — re-living the trauma over and over again, including having physical symptoms like a racing heart or sweating and frightening thoughts. Re-experiencing symptoms may cause problems in a person's everyday routine: just words, objects, or situations that are reminders of the traumatic event, can trigger re-experiencing.

2. Avoidance symptoms: staying away from places, events, or objects that are reminders of the experience. For example, after a bad car accident, a person who usually drives may avoid driving or riding in a car.

3. Hyper-arousal symptoms: being easily startled, feeling tense or "on edge", having difficulty sleeping and/or having angry outbursts. Hyper-arousal symptoms are usually continuous, instead of being triggered by things that remind one of the traumatic events. They can make the person feel stressed and angry. These symptoms may make it hard for the patient to perform daily tasks.

It's natural to have some of the symptoms after a dangerous event and people may have very serious symptoms that go away after a few weeks. This is called acute stress disorder, or ASD. But, when the symptoms last more than a few weeks and become an ongoing problem, the persons might have PTSD.

In addition to the symptoms described above, PTSD patients also suffer from bad depression and sadness, anxiety and Alcohol or drug addictions. The

Alcohol and drugs are used to still the "demons" that continuously haunt them. Patients may also feel suicidal. The memorable portrayal of a crippled and Alcoholic Vietnam war veteran, "lieutenant Dan", portrayed by actor Gary Sinise in "Forrest Gump", is an excellent illustration of a PTSD stricken war veteran who at one time in the movie wanted to commit suicide."

After they read all they could, John told his team: "dear friends, as you know, many PTSD patients also have drug abuse problems. However, when we run our trial, we will choose patients without drug problems. Thus we will be able to study the SOMA's effect on PTSD alone, dissociated from drug addiction. However, regardless of whether the SOMA will or will not cure PTSD, our next trial will tackle drug addiction."

John and his team contacted the Winchester center's director, Dr. William Trent and described to him their past successes with the mental disorders that they had already studied so far. Dr. Trent was very happy to start a trial with what seemed like to him like an excellent psychiatric drug. John asked Dr. Trent to enroll only patients who are free of drug addictions (verifiable by repeated urine tests) explaining that he eventually plans to run a separate clinical trial on Heroin addicts that do not suffer from PTSD.

When starting to plan the trial, Dr. Trent suggested that it will contain three arms: one group of patients will receive SOMA inhalers and undergo their regular psychiatric treatment sessions; another group will receive placebo inhalers and will also undergo the same psychiatric treatment, and the third group will receive placebo inhalers and will be treated with the psychiatric Prolonged Exposure (PE) method developed by Professor Edna Foa. He said that Professor Foa from the University of Pennsylvania's Center for the Treatment and Study of Anxiety and the Department of Psychiatry in the School of Medicine, developed a successful therapy for PTSD patients that involved identifying the thoughts and situations that had triggered fear in each patient, and then gently exposing the patients to those situations: the patients are asked to summon up the memories and the images associated with the trauma more and more vividly. Following that, the patients are gently exposed to films of combat or car accidents or any other frightening situation that triggered their PTSD. The facing of the frightening memories and images gradually striped them of their debilitating power. The approach works fast—usually within a structured program of 12 sessions. The patients are also provided with education about PTSD and are taught a breathing control method for helping them to manage anxiety.

Dr. Trent told the team that the US Department of Veterans Affairs had put Professor Foa's treatment protocol into wide use and that it is now implementing programs to teach it to mental health therapists of the VA across the various services.

John said: "Dr. Trent, if Professor Foa's approach is so successful, why do you need the SOMA?"

Dr Trent answered: "We need the SOMA, hopefully, for two reasons: many PTSD patients are very reluctant to open old wounds that are a must in Foa's method and also, much more importantly, we need to treat many thousands of patients, but I have in my clinic at present only three qualified therapists who had attended Professor Foa's courses. No, a drug which will cure every one of the many thousands of PTSD veteran patients in the country without a need for hundreds of qualified therapists, and without much hassle, is extremely necessary!"

Dr Trent enrolled forty-eight non-addicted PTSD veterans that came regularly to the clinic for psychiatric treatments but, as yet, had not received any PE treatments. These veterans were randomly divided into three groups with an approximately similar division of ages and wars (Vietnam, Iraq and Afghanistan). The groups were assigned the letters "A", "B" or "C." John and his team coded 16 placebo inhalers with the letter "A" and revealed to Dr. Trent and his clinicians that these are placebo inhalers intended for the PE treatment group. Next, they coded sixteen SOMA inhalers with the letter "B" and sixteen additional placebo inhalers with the letter "C." The identities of the "B" and "C" inhalers were withheld from Dr. Trent and his staff. All the psychiatric treatments (PE for group A patients, or conventional – for groups "B" and "C" patients) were to be administered by Dr. Trent's three PE qualified clinicians at a rate of two sessions per week. This way, all 48 patients were to undergo a total of twelve sessions (for thirty-two of them—a regular psychiatric treatment, and for the other sixteen—the twelve sessions required by the PE method). Dr. Trent did not participate in the trial, since he had not taken the PE course and also because he had his usual managerial duties and the task of supervising the whole trial. John asked Dr. Trent to enroll his dad as one the 16 patients of "B" or "C" groups. He told his dad that he may not feel any improvement in the six weeks of the trial, since he has a 50% chance of being placed in the placebo group. But he told his dad that if the SOMA will work, he will be entitled, officially, to receive the SOMA after the end of the trial. John's father was already well aware of his son's previous successes with the SOMA and willingly joined the trial.

At the end of each week of the trial, John and his team, and Dr. Trent and his clinicians met for a follow-up session. Starting with the first week, the three clinicians, without knowing the identity of the "B" or "C" groups, described an amazing progress in group B patients – they were happier, serene and reported a general improvement in all mental aspects of their life. The patients of the PE Group "A" exhibited a certain regression in their mental condition at the start, but this was expected in the PE treatment due to the surfacing of all the experiences they had tried so hard to suppress (a real improvement in Professor Foa's method, is expected to appear only after 8 or 9 sessions). Group "C" placebo patients expected an improvement in their condition because of the trial, and therefore reported a slight placebo-like improvement. But this "improvement" had soon dissipated as the trial went on. As a result, Dr. Trent and his clinicians said that they believe that they already know the exact identity of groups "B" and "C" members, but did not press John to break the code.

The results of the clinical trial were tremendously successful. Most PE patients reported a strong improvement; the SOMA patients were cured and were both ecstatic and serene, while the placebo patients remained with their unresolved PTSD. At the end of the trial, all forty-eight patients, including those who recovered as a result of the PE treatment, received SOMA inhalers for one month and were told that they will routinely receive a new inhaler at the beginning of each month for one year (John left enough inhalers for a whole year's supply with Dr. Trent, hoping that the SOMA will be certified by the FDA after one year). The patients also received the usual Ben's concocted warning. Only one year later, when the SOMA was openly distributed to the whole world, they understood the reason for the warnings that they had received. . .

19

Year 2013

While the PTSD trial was still progressing, John assembled his team and said: "Dear colleagues, the time has come for us to try to abolish drug addiction. Our next trial will be carried out on Heroin abusers that are trying to undergo a "drying-out" process in one of the Drug Dependency Treatment Centers in Boston. Now, I will have you know that I have served for a while as a Pharmacology expert in a special committee for drug abuse and treatment which had been established by the governor of Massachussettes and therefore I studied the Heroin addiction problem quite extensively. It is true that we have committees, programs and centers galore all over the country. However, Heroin addiction is most difficult to eradicate, even with replacement therapies with drugs such as Methadone and Buprenorphine. Both of these drugs alleviate Heroin's very torturous withdrawal symptoms. But the wish to reexperience Heroin "highs" is still present, and it takes a very strong-willed individual to resist the psychological urge to regress back to addiction. All addictive drugs, including Heroin and Alcohol (which we will tackle later in another clinical trial), stimulate a reward circuit in the brain. The circuit provides incentives for abuse by registering the rewarding and pleasurable experiences through the release of the dopamine, telling the brain "to do it again." Therefore, what makes permanent recovery difficult are drug-induced changes that create lasting memories linking the drug to a pleasurable reward.

When I started my tenure as adviser to the governor's committee, I asked my dad what he knew about drug abuse in Vietnam, which was the harbinger of the Heroin abuse of to-day. He told me that Marijuana, Amphetamines, Opium and Heroin were almost openly used in Vietnam without any extensive legal persecution by the army. In a battalion-briefing on drug abuse among soldiers that he attended in 1968 with his fellow officers, they were told that 50 percent of American servicemen "do" drugs and the officers were given instructions to try to fight this problem. American intelligence sources received many reports that the Vietcong secretly exported drugs into the south in order to undermine American morale and their wish to fight. Notoriously similar technics were used by England, and other western countries using opium smuggling into China, during their attempt to open trade with her, by force. By the year 1970, when my Dad was released from the army, the percentage of drug users among servicemen had jumped to 65%. My Dad also said that drugs in Vietnam were both cheap and easily available and were a way for the soldiers to escape from the anxiety and stress of combat. He told me that in 1967 opium cost 1 dollar, while morphine was sold for 5 dollars per vial. Tablets of Binoctal, an addictive drug, were sold at 1—to 5—dollars for twenty tablets. Heroin was widely available to U.S troops and was smoked (not injected) in the following way: a regular cigarette was rolled between the finger and thumb to loosen its tobacco. After the cigarette was partially emptied, a vial containing 250 milligrams of 94 to 96 percent pure heroin liquid was poured into it. Often, the widespread heroin use among U.S. servicemen in Vietnam was caused by starting with marijuana and then "graduating" to heroin abuse.

Heroin is processed from morphine, a naturally occurring substance extracted from the seed pods of certain varieties of poppy plants. It is typically sold as a white or brownish powder, or as a black sticky substance known in the streets as "black tar heroin." Although purer heroin is becoming more common, most street heroin is "cut" with other drugs or with substances such as sugar, starch, powdered milk, or quinine. Heroin causes a very strong and rapid surge in the levels of the three neurotransmitters which affect the reward system in the brain, thereby causing addiction. The brain remembers this pleasure and wants it repeated.

The addicts' need to obtain Heroin becomes more important than any other need, including truly vital necessities like eating. The drive to seek and use the drug is all that matters, despite devastating consequences. Finally, self control, freedom of choice and everything that once held value in a person's life—family, job and community—are lost to addiction. As addiction sets in, several changes occur in the brain. The most significant among them is a reduction in the production of the pleasure receptors in the brain. As a result, the addict is incapable of feeling any pleasure, even when he greatly increases his Heroin intake. If Heroin's use is reduced or stopped abruptly, grave withdrawal symptoms occur. These withdrawal symptoms occur within a few hours after the drug was stopped and include restlessness, muscle and bone pain, insomnia, diarrhea, vomiting, cold flashes with goose bumps and involuntary leg movements. The withdrawal symptoms peak between 24 and 48 hours after the last dose and subside after about a week. Heroin withdrawal is never fatal to otherwise healthy adults, but it causes a great deal of suffering.

One of the greatest risks of being a Heroin addict is death from heroin overdose. As a result of the fact that with time, "normal" doses of Heroin fail to induce pleasure, addicts continuously increase their uptake. Consequently, about one percent of all heroin addicts in the United States die each year from an overdose of Heroin, despite their development of fantastic tolerance to high concentrations of the drug.

Because many heroin addicts, including whores, often share needles and injection equipment, they are at a special risk of contracting HIV, Hepatitis and other infectious diseases and passing them on. Drug abuse is the fastest growing vector for the spread of HIV and Hepatitis in the Nation.

How can an addict achieve drug abstinence and overcome the hump of withdrawal symptoms? It is possible to stop "cold turkey" – that is without the help of withdrawal drugs – but, it creates very painful withdrawal symptoms. Another mode of relieving the withdrawal symptoms of Heroin addicts at the start of abstinence is to sedate them heavily for 2-4 days.

At present, the best mode of treatment of Heroin addiction and dependence consists of creating a sort of "narcotic blockade" that stops the craving for the drug. This so called "maintenance agonist treatment" uses one or the other of two medications (agonists) called Methadone and Buprenorphine. These two medications have cross tolerance with Heroin and Morphine and a long duration effect. Both Methadone and Buprenorphine work equally well.

Let us start with the description of Methadone treatment: high doses of methadone can block the euphoric effects of heroin, morphine and similar drugs and can also prevent withdrawal symptoms. As a result, properly—dosed methadone patients who persist in the maintenance of the agonist treatment can overcome the painful withdrawal symptoms and later can also resist their craving.

Methadone maintenance therapy has many years of proven efficacy. It increases overall survival, treatment retention and employment. It decreases Heroin use, criminal activity, prostitution and hepatitis/HIV infections. The treatment is given in clinics and involves daily dosing and nursing assessments, weekly individual and/or group counseling, random urine screenings and psychiatric services. These daily visits to the clinic can be very tiresome to treated addicts. However, individuals can eventually earn 'take-home' doses for a whole week if they have met the goals of the program long enough.

Buprenorphine is the second maintenance therapy drug: it has been shown to be just as effective as methadone in terms of abstinence, continuation of treatment and decreased craving.

The choice between Methadone and Buprenorphine depends on the addict's situation. If he needs a constantly supportive structure, methadone is the better choice. As I have already told you, the goal of both drugs is to alleviate acute craving, but the patients will still continue to crave Heroin, since they remember the acute pleasure they felt at the start of their addiction.

I am fairly certain that the SOMA will prevent addicts from sliding back into abuse, since they can now actually gain pleasure in a safe and easy administration route. They will be able to obtain the SOMA free of charge from the DEA once it is certified. The SOMA will also have an additional advantage, since its pleasure-inducing ability will not diminish over time and will not cause any adverse side-effects."

John finished his long tirade, picked up the phone and asked Dr. Trent to recommend a Drug Dependency Treatment Center in the Boston area. Dr. Trent suggested that they should try the VA Substance Abuse outpatient Treatment Service in Channel Street which specializes in Methadone treatment. Dr. Trent also said that he will call the center's manager, Dr. Perez, who is a friend of his and will prepare the ground for them.

As soon as John put down the phone, which was in a speaker mode, Ben remarked that "It looks like all the psychiatrists and psychologists in Boston seem to be entwined in a "Mafia-style" network where a friend brings a friend." John laughed and reminded Ben that he, John, also belongs to the same Mafia and warned him to behave, or else he will find a decapitated horse head in his bedroom as a result of his insult to the "psychologists' Mafia" . . .

John and his team met Dr. Perez in the latter's office, described their successful results with the SOMA and offered to carry out a trial with him. Dr. Perez, already briefed by Dr. Trent, immediately agreed and they started to discuss the way to perform the trial.

A few days later, Dr. Perez assembled 42 Methadone-treated veterans in the clinic's conference room and said: "men and women veterans; The course you are taking now with Methadone is not easy and I know that you constantly have to fight the urge to slide back to Heroin abuse to regain at least a temporary pleasure. But now your agonies may be over. I have met a group of brilliant scientists from Harvard University who have developed a new, marvelous, addiction-free and pleasure-inducing drug that will replace both Heroin and Methadone. I have invited you to-day to participate in a trial with this new drug. Those who would consider taking part please stay and I will describe the new drug and will answer any questions you may want to ask. You also need to know that, as is the custom in clinical trials, half of you will receive the new drug and the other half will receive a placebo. However, if the drug will work, as I am sure it will, all of you, including the placebo group people, will receive the drug free of charge for a whole year." All present, without any exception, agreed to enroll in the trial and signed informed consent forms. Dr. Perez patiently answered all their questions and then said: "The drug or the placebo will be administered with an inhaler of the same type used by asthma patients. You will take one whiff per day from your inhaler which delivers only a single, but accurate, dose per day when you press the piston. Later I will demonstrate to you the correct method of inhalation using a placebo inhaler. Both the true drug and the placebo will suffice exactly for one month. In addition, those of the placebo group will receive enough Methadone doses for one month to take together with the inhalers, whereas the real new drug takers will receive placebo doses that look and taste exactly like Methadone. You will report back to the clinic after one month and will be interviewed about your experience with the drug. You may tell your families about the trial, but you will need to swear them to secrecy. It is very important that you should not tell any of your friends about the trial and don't let them try the inhaler which contains an exact number of whiffs for one month. If you let anybody else use the inhaler, you will miss doses at the end of the month and will suffer very painful withdrawal symptoms from the lack of the drug.

Dr. Perez demonstrated the correct use of the inhaler and put the list of the coded SOMA or placebo users in his safe.

The trial was extremely successful. The scientists and Dr. Perez knew that they have gained, at last, an extremely important victory in the war against drug addiction. Although John and his team had only tested Heroin addiction, they were quite sure that the SOMA will also work on all abuse drugs in general, since almost all illegal street drugs work with the same type of receptor as that of Endorphin and Heroin. Thus John and his team added a very important "scalp" to the collection that they have accumulated so far on their belts . . .

20

Year 2013

Several days after the successful completion of the Heroin trial, John assembled his team and said: "Dear colleagues, our next clinical trial will be on Alcohol, which I consider to be even more destructive than Heroin. I am sure that each of you had met Alcoholic friends or poor drunks in the street, stumbling along with bottles of "booze" in paper bags and mumbling to themselves. The World Health Organization estimates that there are 140 million Alcoholics worldwide. In the US, as many as 15 million people, of whom 5 million are women, are addicted to it at any given time. Women are more sensitive than men to Alcohol's deleterious physical, cerebral and mental effects. Alcohol damages almost every organ in the body including the brain. Because of the cumulative toxic effects of chronic Alcohol abuse, alcoholics risk suffering from a wide range of medical and psychiatric disorders. Alcoholism has profound social consequences for the alcoholics themselves and the people of their lives. It is a disabling addictive disorder and, as with other drugs, an Alcohol abuser will increase the amount of the Alcohol that he consumes, because gradually increasing alcohol concentrations become necessary to obtain the same level of euphoria as at the start. The long-term Alcohol abuse can cause a number of physical symptoms such as cirrhosis of the liver, epilepsy, Alcoholic dementia, heart disease, nutritional deficiencies, sexual dysfunction and can, eventually be fatal. Addicts may also stand the risk of developing cardiovascular disease and cancer. Approximately 10 percent of all dementia cases are related to Alcohol consumption, making it the second leading cause of dementia after Alzheimer's disease.

On hearing John's frightening descriptions, Debbie said: "I used to read in the Old Testament as a girl, and when you talked about destructive effects, a passage from Proverbs popped into my head: a father admonishes his son to stay away from loose women saying "Many are the victims she has brought down; her slain are a mighty throng." It was not my intention to make any hints, John . . . but this description certainly applies very well to Alcohol!"

John smiled and said: "Right, Debbie, I got your point about loose women . . . But, don't you worry; you are all the women that I will ever want, rolled into one.

Now, in a more serious vein – in preparation for a clinical trial with Alcoholics I studied several sources, and here is the gist of what I learned: First, how does Alcohol induce pleasure and addiction? Alcohol performs its action through 3 mechanisms:

Through Endorphin: Alcohol raises endorphin levels. This reduces pain and leads to a pleasurable endorphin "high."

Through Dopamine: Alcohol raises dopamine levels. This increase leads to excitement and stimulation and also to the entrenchment of dependence by enhancing memories of the pleasure experiences. As I have already told you when we started our Heroin trial, addictive drugs, and this also applies to Alcohol, stimulate a reward circuit in the brain. The circuit provides incentives for more Alcohol consumption by registering its pleasure and rewarding experiences. These experiences tell the brain "to do it again." What makes permanent recovery difficult is an alcohol-induced change that creates lasting memories linking the drug to a pleasurable reward.

Through Serotonin: In addition to inducing pleasure and serenity, studies have demonstrated that Alcohol directly stimulates the brain to produce the pleasure–inducing serotonin. Serotonin, just like Dopamine, is also involved in the brain's reward system and plays an important role in Alcohol abuse.

Our SOMA binds to the same opiate receptors as those of alcohol but with greater affinity and thus will prevent Alcohol from attaching to the receptors. But much more than that—our SOMA will induce pleasure, euphoria and serenity without hang-overs and without the terrible effects of Alcohol on a person's health and brain.

Withdrawal from Alcohol is difficult and may require medical supervision. The treatment may involve the use of withdrawal medications that are given under the care of a physician to ensure that the transition from active addiction to active recovery is achieved without harm or unnecessary discomfort. As I have already mentioned, Alcohol is a drug that produces both tolerance and the need for increasing quantities to achieve desired results. When its use is discontinued, it may cause dangerous withdrawal symptoms. For persons suffering from Alcohol dependence or addiction, the withdrawal symptoms can be much worse than those of Heroin withdrawal and may require supervised medical care. The greatest danger in Alcohol withdrawal is the potential for life-threatening seizures accompanied by delirium. In the worst cases, physicians utilize a technic called a "taper" to help the withdrawing person through the worst of the symptoms during withdrawal, and to protect him or her from seizures. A "taper" is usually accomplished by administering a sedative such as Phenobarbital whose dosages are gradually reduced until there is no further danger of seizure. In order to maintain abstinence after the "taper", physicians use one of two drugs that I will describe later. If withdrawal is to be effective, medical treatment is also accompanied with psychosocial counseling, education on the nature of addiction and on recovery. Such counseling is efficiently provided by the "Alcoholics Anonymous" organization. As with all forms of addiction, Alcohol dependence is a chronic problem with the ever present threat of relapse. In fact, Alcohol dependence is incurable in that the user can never completely return to non-addicted state. But, his dependence can be brought into long-term or even permanent remission through abstinence.

Treatment for Alcohol abstinence withdrawal clinics is carried out in with one of two drugs: Naltrexone and Disulfiram.

Naltrexone is an opioid receptor antagonist. It works by binding to opioid receptors, thus blocking them off so that all drugs, including Alcohol, cannot bind to them and cannot induce pleasure.

Disulfiram acts by preventing the elimination of acetaldehyde, a chemical that is produced during alcohol-breakdown in the body. Acetaldehyde itself is the cause of hangover symptoms following excessive Alcohol use. The increase of acetaldehyde caused by Disulfiram creates severe discomfort when Alcohol is ingested: an extremely fast-acting and long-lasting uncomfortable hangover. This discourages Alcoholics from drinking significant amounts while they take Disulfiram.

Now, as in many instances before, I have already laid the ground for the trial. I spoke with Dr. Perez and he recommended that I will get in touch with Dr. Ann Hertz, the manager of the Edgecombe Psychiatric Hospital in Brookline, MA, that treats drug addicts, including Alcoholics. Needless to say, as a result of Dr. Perez's introductory discussion with Dr. Hertz, she immediately enrolled all her alcohol addicted patients in the trial, after obtaining from them signed informed consent forms."

The trial was carried out again as a double blind one and was a resounding success. John and his team were again elated, knowing that at one simple swoop and with great ease and elegance they have cured a problem that affected hundreds of millions of addicts ever since the first man in ancient times learned that crushed grapes yielded a juice which could be fermented to yield wine and some anonymous chemist found out how to obtain concentrated alcohol by distillation!

21

Year 2013

After hearing about the team's success with PTSD patients, Heroin and Alcohol addicts from Drs. Trent, Perez and Hertz, Enid called John and arranged a meeting with him and his team. In the meeting Enid said:

"Dear friends, you have been marvelously successful with the SOMA till now, obtaining a 1.000 batting average. I challenge you now to start a new trial and believe me, you could not choose a worthier one: let us try to treat autism. This affliction is very distressing both to the patients and to their parents. There are even recorded cases where old parents killed their autistic son or daughter so as not to leave them alone in an uncaring world after their demise, and then committed suicide." John and his colleagues nodded their heads in commiseration and immediately agreed to start an autism trial.

Enid said: "Although the autistic spectrum of disorders is extensive and of varying severity, I think that we stand a good chance to help at least some autistic patients. Since neurotransmitters are vitally important for the control of cognition and behavior, many scientists have pursued the study of the relationship of various neurotransmitters to autism. Several studies have shown that the level of Serotonin in the brain of autistic patients is connected to the severity of the symptoms. It was found that high levels of Serotonin relieve the autistic behaviors of self-harm or withdrawal, which are apparently caused by an increased Noradrenalin level. Here are some examples of the studies:

1. Tryptophan, which is required for the synthesis of Serotonin, was eliminated from the diet of autistic patients by omitting all proteins and replacing them with a tryptophan-free drink of amino acids' solution. This elimination of Tryptophan resulted in an increase in the autistic symptoms of whirling, flapping, rocking, depression and self-injurious behavior among many test subjects.

2. Researchers found a tri-peptide that stimulates the destruction of Serotonin in the brains of 60% of all tested autistic children, thus decreasing Serotonin's availability to the children.

3. The levels of serotonin in the brain change during development: Serotonin synthesis in three to eight year old healthy children, is three times higher than that measured in adults. In three to eight year old autistic children, serotonin synthesis values were only two times higher than those of adult values.

John, you let me read a preprint of your paper on the "Endorphin to Serotonin pathway" and I was very impressed. On the basis of this finding, you must agree with me that autism may be a good candidate for SOMA therapy since it reduces Noradrenalin levels and increases Serotonin levels in the brain."

John said: "Yes, Enid, I agree with you. However, I want you to note that because the Autistic spectrum of disorders is so complex and its mechanisms are still obscure, I believe that we may obtain a partial relief only and that, probably, in only some of the children. So, with this word of caution, let us start the trial. We actually owe it to the patients and their parents."

As soon as Enid secured John's agreement to the trial, she proceeded to enlighten Debbie and Lucia about autism (John and Ben were already familiar with the disorder):

"Autism is one of the most common developmental disabilities. It affects people of every race, ethnic group and socioeconomic background. Boys are four times more likely to have autism than are girls. Autism spectrum disorders affect an average of 0.9% of all eight-year old children.

Autism varies in its severity and the age at which a child may first exhibit symptoms. It is typically diagnosed during a child's second year and is, unfortunately, a life-long disorder, although its symptoms may lessen over time. So far, there is no cure for autism, but appropriate treatments can help a child to develop skills which will enable him to function a little more independently in life.

The word "autism" has its origin in the Greek word "autos," which means "self." Children with severe autism are often self-absorbed and seem to exist in a private world out of which they are unable to communicate and interact with others. They may have difficulty in developing language skills and in understanding what others say to them. They may also have difficulty communicating nonverbally such as through hand gestures, eye contact and facial expressions.

Not every autistic child has a language problem. A child's ability to communicate will vary depending upon his or her intellectual and social development. Some children with autism cannot speak. Others may have rich vocabularies and may be able to talk about specific subjects in great detail. Most children with autism have little or no problem pronouncing words. However, the majority of them have difficulty using language effectively, especially when they talk to other people. Many have problems with the meaning and rhythm of words and sentences, and they are unable to understand body language and the nuances of vocal tones.

Often, children with autism who can speak will say things that have no meaning or that seem out of context. For example, a child may count repeatedly from one to five. Or, a child may continuously repeat words he or she has heard, a condition called "echolalia." Immediate echolalia occurs when the child repeats words someone has just said. For example, the child may respond to a question by asking the same question. In delayed echolalia, the child will repeat words heard at an earlier time. Also, the child may say "do you want something to drink?" whenever he or she want a drink.

Sensory integration and emotional behavior may also be affected. Autistic children may be withdrawn and react unusually to other people, engage in repeated body movements such as hand flapping, or display an unusual attachment to selected objects. They may also be aggressive toward others or to themselves, and often have a marked resistance to changes in routine.

Sensory integration in autistic patients is often very poor so that only one type of sense can be processed at a time. For example, if a patient is looking at something, he or she may not notice that a fire alarm is ringing, or that someone is calling his/her name.

Some children with autism speak in a high-pitched or singsong voice or use robot-like speech. Other children with autism may use stock phrases to start a conversation: a child may say "My name is Tom," even when he talks with friends or family. Still others may repeat what they heard on television programs or commercials.

Some children may be able to deliver an in-depth monologue about a topic that holds their interest, even though they may not be able to carry a two-way conversation about the same topic. Approximately 10 percent of children with autism show "savant" skills, i.e., high abilities in specific areas such as calendar calculation, music, or math. All patients with these savant skills have an amazing memory that is focused in one area only. Their most common behaviors are obsessive preoccupations with trivia (facts about U.S. presidents, license plate numbers, maps, or other obscure items).

The film "Rainman" from 1988 described an autistic person with savant skills ('Raymond', played by Dustin Hoffman). Raymond had a superb recall, but little understanding of subject matter. He was frightened by change and adhered to strict routines (for example, his continual repetition of the "Who's on First?" sketch). Except when he was in distress, he showed little emotional expression and avoided eye contact."

Enid told John and his team that she herself does not treat autistic patients. Therefore she told him to contact the Bernkopf Family Autism Center at Massachusetts General Hospital for Children. As usual, she knew some of the people in the center (they, too, belonged to her Mafia . . .).

Enid and the SOMA team met Dr. Amanda Bergman who headed the center. As was the case in earlier trials, Dr. Bergman was also very eager to try the SOMA on her patients after hearing Enid's preparatory description of the SOMA's successes. She proudly described the program used in her center for treating autistic children called "LADDERS"—short for "Learning and Developmental Disabilities Evaluation & Rehabilitation Services." She said that LADDERS is a multidisciplinary program designed to evaluate and treat autistic children, adolescents and adults with autism. She also said that LADDERS' clinicians developed a comprehensive evaluation and rehabilitation plan for each individual patient which can be implemented by the care-giver or parent or referring physician. This plan provides a long-term follow-up care via periodic consultations and regular re-assessments.

John asked: "Dr, Bergman, how are we going to evaluate whether the SOMA helped the patients? Dr Bergman said: "Well, we will use CARS" and Debbie asked innocently: "How is a car going to help us?" Dr. Bergman laughed and said: "Ha, this is a stock joke among experts dealing with autistic patients. I hoped that at least one of you will fall for it. CARS, short for Childhood Autism Rating Scale, is a behavior rating scale intended to diagnose autism and to follow the progress of autistic patients. CARS had taken 10 years to develop and is considered to be the "gold standard" in the field of autists' rating. It diagnoses autistic children and adults by subjective observations performed by a clinician, a parent, or a teacher. In order to determine of progress of an autistic child, or the lack of it, over time, it ought to be carried out by the same observer, if possible. Rating is performed for 15 different criteria, yielding a composite score. The higher the score, the more severe is the degree of autism. Each of the fifteen criteria is rated with a score of:

1—Normal for the child's age,
2—Mildly autistic,
3—Moderately autistic,
4—Severely autistic.

The scale has a cutoff of 30: the child is autistic if he scores above 30. The maximum score is 60 for the most severe autism. A score of 15 is the best score for normal children.

The criteria tested in CARS are as follows: relationship to people, imitation ability, emotional response, body use, object use, adaptation to change, visual response, listening response, taste-smell-touch response and use, fear and nervousness, verbal communication, non-verbal communication, activity level, level and consistency of intellectual response and general impressions."

John said: "Fine, it is settled then. Let me just point out one slight problem in the administration of the drug that we can easily solve: in our usual clinical trials, the SOMA or placebo is administered to the patients with an inhaler. But, most probably, it may be difficult to teach some of the children how to use it. Therefore, we will supply the SOMA or placebo in a liquid formulation that can be fed with a spoon. The bottles with the solutions will be coded with different numbers. This way, the parents in their homes or the nurses and caretakers in hostels and all your other CARS evaluators will not know what the patients are receiving." Dr. Bergman then said that the trial will not start simultaneously with all the patients in the same day, but would be carried out intermittently, depending on the arrival dates of the patients in the center. The patients' parents or care-givers will be asked to rate the patients at the start of the trial and then again after one month and to return to the center with both assessment results.

The trial consisted of 102 patients randomly dispersed among ages and with about similar severity levels. It took about 3 months for all the results to accumulate.

All those involved in the trial, including the parents and care-givers, eagerly waited for the breaking of the code and for the summing up of the results. Even before the opening of the code, Dr. Bergman happily informed John and his team that from the continuously accumulating CARS results she perceives that something unusual is happening – something that she has never seen before! She also said that the same feeling was echoed by many of the parents and care-givers when they reported back to the clinic.

On opening the code, it was found that improvements were indeed observed in almost all SOMA takers and by none of the placebo takers. The greatest improvement was observed in mildly autistic patients – they have exhibited a mean reduction in CARS rating of 10.7 points. The moderate and severe patients exhibited a mean reduction of 7.2 and 3.9 points, respectively. No improvement was observed in the placebo patients. Dr Bergman said that the greatest improvements occurred in the CARS criteria of verbal communication, relationship to people, fear and nervousness and adaptation to change. John said that, possibly, the increase in Serotonin's concentration in the brain caused a repair or enhanced activity of some garbled neural communication pathways in the patients' brains. Dr. Bergman said that she will be waiting for the approval of the SOMA so that she and all the clinicians in the world will be able, at long last, to really improve the condition of autistic patients.

22

Year 2013

The scientists just barely had time to digest their unexpected success with the autistic children, when they had to confront a new request from the energetic and gently persuasive Enid: "Dear friends, did any of you have a chance to see Alzheimer patients?"

John answered also for his team and said: "Yes; you may recall that I have told you that after our anorectic trial we have performed a trial with elderly frail inmates of the "Amity nursing home" in Boston. That trial did not include any Alzheimer patients, since we had already intended at that time to perform a separate Alzheimer trial later on. Yes, all of us vividly remember those patients who were in various stages of disintegration. We also discussed among us the terrible plight of the patients who were once a whole world unto themselves and to their loved ones, and are now but empty extinguished husks devoid of any humanity. By all means, let us do the trial."

Enid immediately started to enlighten Debbie and Lucia on Alzheimer's disease although, as a result of their trauma at the Amity nursing home, they had already done some reading on the subject:

"Similar to the rest of our bodies' organs, the capabilities of our brains change with time. At old age, most of us detect changes in our thinking speed and in our ability to remember names or phone numbers. However, a serious memory-loss, confusion and big changes in the way our brain works, are not a normal part of the aging process. Such large changes are a sign that our neurons are failing at a fast rate, leading to dementia. Dementia is a general term for the loss of memory and intellectual abilities that are so serious that they cause a disruption in life management. Alzheimer's disease (AD) is the most common form of dementia and is responsible for 50-70% of all dementia cases.

The brain possesses several communication networks. Some of these networks deal with thinking, learning and remembering, whereas others control various organs in the body. In AD, like in other forms of dementia, an increasing number of neurons degenerate and die. AD is termed after a German physician, Dr. Alzheimer, who first described it in a scientific convention as the "case of Mrs. Augusta", a woman he treated in 1901, which suffered from problems in memory, unbased suspicions that her husband betrays her with another woman, problems in speech, and inability to understand when spoken to. Her symptoms progressively became worse; she had to stay in bed all the time, until her death in 1906. Since Dr. Alzheimer never saw such symptoms before, he asked the family for permission to perform an autopsy. In the post-mortem cutting of the brain he saw a dramatic shrinking of the cerebral cortex, the part that is now known to be responsible for memory, judgment and speech. In microscopic examination of brain slices he saw fatty sediments in the brain's capillaries, dead or dying neurons and abnormal sediments in, or around the neurons.

Two abnormal formations observed in Alzheimer brains, are the main suspects of causing AD. These formations are called "plaques" and "tangles." Dr. Alzheimer already saw them in Mrs. Augusta's brain slices, although he termed them differently. Plaques accumulate between neurons and contain large quantities of a proteinaceous molecule called Amyloid Beta Peptide. The tangles, on the other hand, are made of aggregates of a protein called TAU and are found inside dying neurons. Most scientists believe that the plaques and tangles interfere with the communication between neurons and with processes which are essential to their normal function. All healthy persons produce a certain amount of plaques and tangles in their brains as they grow old; but AD patients produce much larger amounts. This accumulation advances in a predictable course which starts in brain areas important to learning and remembering and then spreads to other areas, including those that are in charge of the basic functions of the body such as breathing and heart-beat. However, this final stage of the loss of breathing and heart-beat may not be reached: most of the patients die earlier because of infections caused by wrong food ingestion to the lungs, or by their inserted urinary catheter. Recent statistics in the USA have shown that, at present, over 5 million men and women (i.e., about 2% of the population) suffer from the disease. This number is expected to reach 13.4 million by 2050. Health experts estimate that 65 year old American men or women have a 10% risk of developing AD. At present, it is not possible to cure AD, but it is hoped that the accelerated research which is carried around the world, would lead to the development of drugs capable of preventing AD, or at least retarding its course. To-date, more than 1000 clinical trials have been conducted in the search of useful drugs.

Biochemical studies on Alzheimer's brains have revealed a number of neurochemical abnormalities. These include decreases in the level of serotonin, disruption of the way electrical charges travel within neurons and a progressive decline in the utilization of glucose which is a reflection of a decline in brain activity. This metabolic decline is quantitated by an imaging technique called "glucose PET" which allows direct observation of the degenerative changes in the brain. In the PET (Positron Emission Tomography) technique, suitably labeled glucose is injected to the brain and the rate of glucose utilization in the various areas of the brain is scanned.

Although the course of Alzheimer's disease is unique for every individual, there are many common symptoms. In the early stages, the most commonly recognized symptom is inability to acquire new memories of recently observed events. As the disease progresses, the symptoms include confusion, irritability and aggression, paranoia, mood swings, language breakdown, long-term memory loss and the general inward withdrawal of the sufferers as their senses decline. The duration of the disease varies. AD develops for an indeterminate period of time before becoming fully apparent. The mean life expectancy following diagnosis is approximately seven to ten years. Fewer than three percent of AD patients live more than fourteen years after diagnosis.

My department houses a world-famous research unit that had already contributed greatly to Alzheimer's research. Scientists in this unit were the first to discover 4 genes active in the induction of a form of familial Alzheimer that accounts for about 30% of the total cases of the disease. These genes apparently cause the synthesis of a large amount of Beta Amyloid."

John said: "Dear Enid, I hope that we will be able to improve, even slightly, the patients' conditions although I am a bit skeptical. After all, we know that the Alzheimer brain is badly damaged and is biologically past reconstruction. But, perhaps we will be able to enhance some of the brain's residual communicative ability by increasing the concentration of Endorphin and Serotonin, which are not only pleasure neurotransmitters but are also active in communicability within the brain. The trial will be a double-blind one and the subjects will be fed with SOMA or placebo solutions. Enid, you told us that the patients' condition will be measured with the glucose-PET method. Are there any other tests in addition to the glucose-PET test?

Enid said: "Yes, we also have another yardstick to test AD patients during the trial and that is the MMSE test.

The mini-mental state examination (MMSE), or Folstein test, is a brief 11-point questionnaire used to diagnose and to follow the degree of Alzheimer's impairment. It is used to estimate the severity of cognitive impairment at any time point, and allows us to follow the course of the patients' cognitive changes over time. During a span of about 10 minutes, it tests various functions such as arithmetic, memory and orientation. MMSE includes simple questions in a number of areas such as the time and location of the test, repeating lists of words, arithmetic such as serial-sevens counting, language use and comprehension and basic motor skills.

The interpretation of the MMSE is such that the lower the score obtained, the more severe is the patient's condition. A score between 30 to 24 points indicates that there is no Alzheimer. A score between 23 to18 indicates a mild Alzheimer's impairment and a score between 17 to 0 denotes a severe Alzheimer's impairment.

Enid gave copies of the MMSE questionnaire to John and his team. She also showed them PET scans obtained from normal people and from Alzheimer patients with various degrees of severity, in order to demonstrate both AD's testing methods.

Mini-Mental State Examination (MMSE)

Patient name:_____ Date:_____

Instructions: Ask the questions in the order listed. Score points for each correct response within each question or activity.

Maximum Score	Patient's Score	Questions
5		What is the year? Season? Date? Day of the week? Month?
5		Where are we now: State? County? Town/city? Hospital? Floor?
3		The examiner names three unrelated objects clearly and slowly, then asks the patient to name all three of them. The patient's response is used for scoring. The examiner repeats them until patient learns all of them, if possible. Number of trials: _____
5		I would like you to count backward from 100 by sevens. (93, 86, 79, 72, 65, . . .) Stop after five answers. Alternative: "Spell WORLD backwards" (D-L-R-O-W).
3		Earlier I told you the names of three things. Can you tell me what those were?
2		Show the patient two simple objects, such as a wristwatch and a pencil and ask the patient to name them.
1		Repeat the phrase: "No ifs, ands, or buts."
3		Take the paper in your right hand, fold it in half and put it on the floor. (The examiner gives the patient a piece of blank paper).

1		Please read this and do what it says. (Written instruction is "Close your eyes").
1		Make up and write a sentence about anything. (This sentence must contain a noun and a verb).
1		Please copy this picture." (The examiner gives the patient a blank piece of paper and asks him/her to draw the symbol below. All 10 angles must be present and two must intersect)
Total: 30		

In spite of certain prior doubts expressed by John, the clinical trial yielded relatively good results: The MMSE mean scores increased, although not by by a large magnitude. The increases were greater for mild AD patients and were quite minimal in severe AD patients. The Glucose–PET scans showed similar improvements. However, both Enid and John knew that these improvements are not permanent, because of the unavoidable relentless increase in Amyloid and Tau depositions in the patients' brains. Enid promised to continue studying the patients for several additional months under a SOMA treatment regimen, in order to see whether the SOMA will cause at least some retardation in the progression of the disease. In spite of the relatively mild improvements, the scientists were satisfied. They felt like kids in a confectionary store trying to sample this or that "goody" (from Schizophrenia to Alzheimr, etc.), even though some goodies were not as tasty as others (Autism and Alzheimer's) .

23

Year 2013

According to the pattern already established by the "pitiless" Enid, John and his team barely had time to rest on their laurels when they were confronted with another of Enid's never ending requests which they pretended to grumble about, but with which, in effect, they were happy to comply. This time Enid begged them to start a trial with Obsessive-Compulsive Disorder (OCD) patients. John and team were somewhat familiar with the disorder but only in a laymen's fashion. Therefore, as was their habit in the past, they read on OCD in the National Institute of Mental Health's site. They learned that OCD is an anxiety disorder which is characterized by recurrent, unwanted thoughts (obsessions) and/or repetitive behaviors (compulsions). Repetitive behaviors such as hand washing, counting, checking, or cleaning are often performed in order to avoid obsessive thoughts or making them go away. Performing these so-called "rituals," however, provides only temporary relief and refraining from performing them markedly increases anxiety.

OCD can be accompanied by eating disorders, other anxiety disorders, or depression. It strikes both men and women in roughly equal numbers and usually appears in childhood, adolescence, or early adulthood. One-third of adults with OCD already develop symptoms in childhood, and research indicates that OCD might run in families.

If people are obsessed with germs or dirt, they may develop a compulsion to wash their hands over and over again. If they develop an obsession with intruders, they may lock and relock their doors many times before going to bed. Being afraid of social embarrassment, may prompt people to comb their hair compulsively many times in front of a mirror until sometimes they get "caught" in the mirror and can't move away from it. Performing such rituals is not pleasurable. At best, it produces temporary relief from the anxiety created by their obsessive thoughts.

Other common rituals are a need to check things repeatedly, touch things (especially in a particular sequence), or to count things. Some common obsessions include having frequent thoughts of committing violence and harming loved ones, persistently thinking about performing sexual acts that the person dislikes, or having thoughts that are prohibited by religious beliefs. People with OCD may also be preoccupied with order and symmetry; they may also have difficulty in throwing things out, so they hoard unneeded items.

Healthy people also have rituals such as checking several times to see if the stove is off before leaving the house. The difference is that people with OCD perform their rituals even though doing them interferes with their daily life and even when they find these repetitions quite distressing.

The course of the disease is quite varied. Symptoms may come and go, ease over time, or get worse. If OCD becomes severe, it can keep a person from working or carrying out normal responsibilities at home. People with OCD may try to help themselves by avoiding situations that trigger their obsessions, or they may use Alcohol or drugs to calm themselves.

OCD responds, to some extent, to treatment with certain drugs and/or exposure-based psychotherapy. These drugs can keep the patients under control while they receive psychotherapy. The principal drugs used for OCD are antidepressants, anti-anxiety drugs and monoamine oxidase inhibitors (MOAIs) which control some of the symptoms, but do not cure them.

John said: "We know, as regular SOMA users, that the SOMA is an excellent anti-anxiety drug. Therefore, my guesss is that it will also work well in OCD." John and team gave Enid all the SOMA and placebo inhalers that she needed for the trial and let her run it all by herself with her staff, knowing that she is quite expert in this kind of bussines. The trial was extremely successful. John took it calmly in his stride being so sure beforhand of the efficacy of their "brain child" for OCD. Familiarity (with success) breeds contempt . . .

As a result of the successes with the SOMA, John considered changing its name to "Cornucopia", since it turned to be is so abundant in its blessings to humanity. Therefore, he gingerly described his suggestion to his friends. They thought about it for a while and then Debbie said: "Why don't we call it "Cur-all-mental", since it cures all mental disorders? The scientists pronounced John's and Debbie's suggestions in order to see how it "feels" and were still undecided. John put an end to their hesitation by leaving the original name of SOMA. .

24

Year 2013

In one of the team's regular meetings, John said: "a few weeks ago, in a discussion with Ben, I raised the possibility that the SOMA will not only raise the happiness and serenity level of all Humanity, but may also improve their physical health by strengthening their immune system.

There is now a growing field called PsychoNeuroImmunology (PNI), which attempts to understand the interactions between the nervous system, the immune system and the psyche. Scientists have found correlations between stress, depression and the immune system.

Having a positive attitude seems to correlate with an increased ability of the immune system to fight disease. Correlations were observed in the number of protecting white blood cells in the blood circulation and a person's level of optimism. The immune system "talks" to our nervous and hormonal systems and vice versa. Stress, dieting, joy, positive thinking, distress, depression, bereavement, fatigue—all affect our immune system.

Hormones regulate the immune system: there are several hormones that are generated by components of the immune system itself. One class of these hormones is called lymphokines. In addition, Corticosteroid hormones (for example Cortisone) and Adrenaline suppress the immune system. On the other hand, Thymosin (thought to be produced by the thymus) is a hormone that encourages white cells' production by the thymus and bone marrow.

People experience many stressors throughout each day and these stressors affect the ability of the immune system to function at the highest possible level. Many important studies have shown that there is a correlation between these stressors and a person's health.

I believe that our SOMA ought to have a very large impact on the immune system by eliminating anxiety, improving mood and alleviating stress. Dear colleagues, what, in your opinion, would be the best way to test the effect of the SOMA on the immune system?"

Debbie quickly raised her hand, as a student who wants to make a comment in class, and John pointed his finger towards her as if graciously giving her permission to speak. Debbie said "The human immune system works through several arms; the more important arms are antibodies and white blood cells such as macrophages and lymphocytes. It seems to me that AIDS patients, whose immune systems are in a bad shape, should be good candidates for study."

John kept an immobile face and said: "Describe and explain why" as if he was testing one of his students in class. Debbie pretended to stammer a little as if in awe of the lecturer, and said: "The CD4+ T lymphocytes in the blood are the main target of HIV virus in infected patients. HIV multiplies in these lymphocytes and destroys them. After some time, if the patients did not respond well to the anti-HIV drug Cocktail, the number of these immune cells decreases and the immune system is greatly weakened. When the CD4+T cell count decreases below a certain level, and the patient will progress from a state of HIV carrier to a state of active AIDS. In this state the patients will develop tumors, or are severely infected with otherwise innocuous "opportunistic" microorganisms. The number of CD4+T lymphocytes in the blood is easily quantitated by a technique called Flow Cytometry. Healthy persons without HIV have about 700 to 1000 CD4+T cells in a microliter of blood. HIV infected people are still considered to have normal CD4+T counts if it is above 500. If the number of these cells drops to below 200, the patient is as diagnosed as having AIDS."

John said: "very well miss, er . . . , Cohen, Right? You will get an A grade not only for your excellent exposition, but also for being my lovely Debbie . . . As usual I have already planned ahead. I contacted Dr. Vincent Büchner who is the director of the Jack T. and Amelia M. Morris Institute in Massachusetts General Hospital. This institute studies various diseases, including AIDS, and is very well-endowed by various philanthropists. As an aside, let me tell you that we are lucky to work in

Boston, since all the excellent hospitals and institutions that we need for our clinical trials are closely situated around us. Needless to say, Dr. Büchner agreed to carry this trial with us. Unlike some other trials, this trial will not be a double-blind one since Dr. Büchner asked me, and I agreed, to give SOMA only, without placebo, to all his patients, on a compassionate basis, since they do not have too much time to waste. He said that he will monitor the patients' medical condition and their CD4+T lymphocyte counts to see if there will be any improvement after the administration of the SOMA."

The trial started and the effect of the SOMA was immediately evident in the patients' moods which were "down" before the administration of the SOMA as a result of their impending doom. Most of the patients also exhibited very nice increases in their CD4+ cell counts after 2 or 3 weeks. Unfortunately, this high count did not eliminate such AIDS-related tumors as Kaposi's Sarcoma once they had become entrenched, but it did eliminate the danger of opportunistic infections such as that of the Pneumocystis fungus or other innocuous infectious agents. John gave Dr. Büchner a large supply of inhalers for his patients in order to prevent their sliding back to the dangerously low CD4+ cell counts.

The extreme case of AIDS patients proved to the scientists that the SOMA has an excellent reinforcing effect on the immune system and will probably improve the health of all its takers.

25

Year 2022

John severed himself from his past silent reminiscences, which concomitantly occupied his mind during his Tri-D address and returned his whole attention to his viewers: "Dear viewers," He said. "Let me recount to you several marvelous stories about events that happened during our SOMA research in 2013, since our younger viewers may not be familiar with them.

The climate in the years of 2011, 2012 and 2013 was very erratic and quite hot or very cold in many regions of the world. In spite of the efforts of the United Nations' Framework Convention on Climate Change and of some of the more responsible nations to reduce the emision of greenhouse gases according to the Kyoto protocol, the average global temperature rose by 0.2 degrees centigrade per year. Peple continued to drive polluting cars, factories continued to emit smoke and the number of cattle and sheep which produce digestive gases grew alarmingly. All of these greenhouse gases—water vapor, carbon dioxide and methane—took their immediate toll. They absorbed the infra-red heat that was emitted from the globe and did not allow it to dissipate to the outside void. As a result, the number of terrifying hurricanes in various locations in the globe rose noticeably, and the aridization in Africa and the thawing of glaciers in the poles increased considerably.

Finally, a ray of hope pierced the darkness. Two billionaires, Bill Kelly and Warren Brooks, convened a press conference in New-York on october 12th 2013 to announce the inauguration of a campaign designed to reduce the content of greenhouse gases in the atmosphere. In this press conference, Bill Kelly, the spokesman, said that their campaign will be carried out by a new non-profit consortium called "Climate" that they have just founded.

Bill Kelly said: "As you know, several years ago, my wife and I have established a welfare foundation with a finance base of many billions of dollars to help victims of catastrophies and poverty. Warren Brooks had since joined the foundation and also brought in a major part of his fortune. The new "climate" consortium is financed by our joint foundation.

Climate's plan, developed by microbiologists whose names we shall withold for the time being, is based on a discovery made in the seventies and eighties of the previous century: the discovery dealt with the biodegradation of oil spills by hydrocarbon-degrading bacteria. The scientists of that time isolated bacteria that grew on the surface of oil slicks in the Gulf of Fos of the French Mediterranean coast. These bacteria, which were able to grow very effectively on crude oil, were used to get rid of oil spills. The bacteria released an enzyme that degraded crude oil and nourished on the hydrocarbons that were released from it.

This phenomenon of the biodegrading bacteria stimulated our group of microbiologists to develop genetically engineered bacteria that released a peptide enzyme capable of synthsizing sugar from the Carbon Dioxide and water vapors in the atmosphere, in a very similar way to the photosynthesis process carried out by plants. To produce this "photosynthesizing peptide enzyme" in large quantities and to disperse it to the atmosphere they came to us for help. As a result, our consortium is now building many factories around the globe to produce large amounts of the peptide enzyme. The enzyme, in the form of dried micropowder, will be used to coat extremely small carbon particles – i.e. nanoparticles. Additional factories will produce billions of inhalers very similar to the Ventolin inhalers used by asthma patients. These inhalers, which will be powered by pressurized air, will be filled with the enzyme nanoparticles. We will distribute the inhalers to every citizen in the world together with 10$ bills as incentive to release the enzyme all over the world. Deserts and arid areas will not be seeded with our peptide enzyme, due to the scarcity of green-house gases or water vapor in their atmosphere. Similarly, the unpoluted ice fields of the north and south poles will also remain unseeded, since their atmosphere lacks appreciable amounts of carbon dioxide. At a certain date, fixed beforehand by our scientists, all citizens of the world will be asked to release the enzyme from the inhalers wherever they live, and as close as possible to factories, city centers and cattle—or sheep-farms. Our ecologists and meteorologists calculated that only billions of streams of the enzyme, released simultaneously all over the world, will create the necessary concenration of enzyme required for the removal, or at least the reduction in the amount of the greenhouse gases in the atmosphere.

This process will have to be repeated every six months. We hope that if "Climate"s method will work, rich countries in the world and perhaps also the UN, will join our consortium and will help us with their financial resources. If the idea won't work, then at least for a while, we have created scores of thousands of jobs around the world."

After Bill Kelly finished, the hundreds of reporters present applauded enthusistically. Even though skeptical by nature and profession they admired the sheer audacity and the huge magnitude of effort of "Climate'"s enterprise. As is their custom in press conferences, many reporters raised their hands for questions. However, Bill Kelly said that he is not going to answer any, saying that if the plan works, all its details will be released. If not, there is no point in answering hypothetical questions beforehand. Bill Kelly and Warren Brooks then waved to the reporters and left.

Our older viewers are familiar with this story and now the younger ones among you also understand that the two billionaires perpetrated a big scam. We and the billionaires knew that before letting the world enjoy the SOMA's breakthrough, it was necessary to produce billions of inhalers that should suffice for all the world's population several times over. The billionaires' scam was so successful that even the production personnel in the SOMA factories had swallowed the story hook, line and sinker.

Two years after their big scam, the two philanthropic billionaires established another consortium called "Climate 2." "Climate 2" really intended this time to try to reduce the content of the greenhouse gases in the atmosphere. The scientists of the new consortium produced nanoparticles coated with an extremely thin layer of platinum metal. Platinum is widely used as a chemical catalyst. For instance, it is used in the catalytic converters that are found in the exhaust systems of most modern cars. Climate 2's platinum nanoparticles were designed to convert the carbon dioxide and water vapors into liquid Carbonic Acid that will not interfer with the dissipation of the globe's heat energy into space. These catalytic nanoparticles were sent to the atmosphere with inter-continental missiles contributed by the world's superpowers with very good results. At start, the liquid Carbonic Acid product caused some Acid Rain, but this rain quickly disappered due to the rapidly decreasing concentrations of Carbon Dioxide in the atmosphere.

'Climate''s biotechnological plants went full steam ahead and continued to produce the billions of inhalers that will be required for the launching of the SOMA. During this production period, the 2 billionaires purchased a pharmceutical company which produced SOMA batches for the clinical trials required to gain FDA's approval for the SOMA. This company also contracted a very large CRO company that carried out the required clinical trials for

Schizophrenia and Major depression. Because of the large sums of money spent in the trials, patients and medical centers were enrolled at top speed and the results of the extensive Schizophrenia and major depression clinical trials flowed in and were excellent. Next, the required extensive paperwork was submitted to the FDA which approved the drug in record time.

With the FDA's certification letters in our pockets we still needed to square things with Harvard with regards to marketing rights and royalties. Therefore, we requested a meeting with Harvard's associate-provost who was the director of the Technology Development Office and with Harvard's provost himself who was, quite by chance, a neurochemistry professor himself. Harvard's Technology Development Office handles all matters dealing with intellectual property, patents and copyrights on inventions made by Harvard's academic and research staffs. A highly trusted lawyer of "Climate" also participated in the meeting. We showed the FDA's letters of approval of the SOMA to the provost and associate provost, and described how the SOMA is going to be distributed free of charge to all humanity. "Climate"'s lawyer said that John and his team had renounced any royalties that they could have gained from the SOMA, but that Bill Kelly and Warren Brooks want to compensate Harvard for its loss of royalty money due to the free dispensing of the SOMA. The provost, who knew John very well (they belonged to the same department), asked john to meet him later in his office to hear all about the development of the SOMA and its marvels. He conferred with his associate-provost and then said that any donations from the billionaires would be welcome, but they are not mandatory, because the invention of the SOMA by a Harvard team would raise Harvard's academic status in the world from sharing the No. 1 position with MIT, to being No.1 alone at the top.

Later that day I conferred with "Climate'"s lawyer and asked him to compensate Lucia for her loss of the royalty money promised to her several months ago. As a result, Lucia received generous monthly bonuses from the 2 billionaires for life, that she, unwillingly, had to share with the **IRS**.

26

Year 2022

"Soon after settling the royalties issue, my team, myself, Bill and Warren obtained an interview with UN secretary Ravi Meenkshee (who replaced Ban Ki Moon at the beginning of 2013), in order to suggest a plan to achieve "ultimate world peace." In the meeting, which also included the Secretary's aides, I described how the SOMA, which is now being now massively produced in 'Climate's factories, is going to turn all the world's citizens into euphoric and serene people who will abhor terrorist activities and wars. We gave the UN secretary and his aides copies of FDA's certification letters and the summaries of our clinical trials which were written by Professor Enid LeBlanc and Drs Benchly, Trent, Perez and Bergman. These summaries described how the SOMA so successfully cured their patients. The clinicians also wrote that they reguarly take the SOMA themselves and how happy and serene they are as a result. I gave an inhaler to each one of the UN executives and asked them to try it, and to grant us another meeting a few days later. We did not have to wait long for the results of our "clinical trial" with the UN people, and three days later Ravi Meenkshee invited us to an additional meeting.

The serene and happy Ravi Meenakshi asked what role we planned for the UN in our peace project. I told him that we would like to enlist the UN's patronage and help in the distribution of the SOMA to the whole world. I also said that by this monopolistic act of distribution, the UN will become the sole powerful world government that will be able to fulfill its prime mandate of bringing peace to the world. I said that by withholding the SOMA from belligerent countries and dictators, the UN will be able to "speak softly and wield a big stick" for the imposition of world-wide peace. Ravi Meenakshi again asked for some time to confer with his aides and two days later we re-convened. The secretary told us that he and most of his staff had been won over to our proposed peace plan, but that there were some people in his staff who were still a bit sketical. The doubters said that the effect of the SOMA on them was marvelous and increased their wish to achieve world peace. However, they expresed doubts as to whether the SOMA will also work on war-like people and terrorists in the various war spots in the world. Meenakshi told us that he has enough authority and votes to adopt our plan, but in order to dispel the doubts of the dissenters and to obtain unanimous agreement, he sugested that the UN itself will test the pacifying effects of the SOMA in some war spot in the world. He suggested the Darfur region in Sudan as a "test case" for the SOMA. He promised that in case of success, he and his whole administration will commit all the resources of the UN to the project. We immediately agreed to this new trial saying that it would indeed serve as a good "test case" for the SOMA.

Ravi Minakshee said: "Very well, then. Let me describe the plan that we have concocted: as you probably know, Sudan had long been plagued by terrible and bloody civil wars and tribal clashes. First, there was a long-running war between Sudan's north and south regions: the Northern Islamic Arab-dominated government fought with southern Christian and animist African rebels over political power, oil and religion. After many international efforts, a peace treaty was finally signed between the Northern and southern regions of Sudan in 2005. Later, in January 2011, a referendum was held in Southern Sudan that resulted in an overwhelming victory for those who wanted to secede from the north. The Khartoum government decided to honor the results and thus Sudan was split into two countries, ending years of bloodshed.

However, in the Darfur region, which is part of Sudan that lies along the western part of Sudan adjacent to the border with Chad, the situation was far from peaceful—a rebellion started in the early 1970's against the central government of Sudan—the Darfurian rebels accused the government of economically neglecting Darfur. It was not clear whether the rebels merely sought to improve their economic position within Sudan, or wanted to achieve outright secession. Both the government and the rebels have been accused of atrocities in this war, but most of the atrocities have been perpetrated by the government-sponsored Muslim Arab militia known as the "Janjaweed." This militia was composed of tribesmen appointed and armed by Al Saddiq Al Mahdi, the former prime minister of Sudan, ostensibly in order to stop the longstanding chaotic disputes between the various Darfurian tribes. However, instead of ending the dispute, the Janjaweed militia has been engaging in genocide: the fighting has displaced hundreds of thousands of people, many of them seeking refuge in neighboring Chad. Most of the top echelon of the Janjaweed is under cover. But, the US State Department suspects that its leader is Musa Hilal, a leader of a small but powerful Darfurian Arab tribe. The government claimed victory over the rebels after capturing a town on the border with Chad in early 1994. However, the fighting resumed in 2003 and it reached such proportions, and the atrocities perpetrated by the Janjaweed militia were so terrible, that it became the worst humanitarian crisis of the 21st century.

On May 5 2006, the Sudanese government and Darfur's largest rebel group, the SLM (Sudanese Liberation Movement), signed a Peace Agreement which aimed at ending the long conflict, and established a temporary government in which the rebels could take part. However, the agreement, which was brokered by the African Union, was not signed by all of rebel groups. A new rebel group called the National Redemption Front has emerged that wanted to secede from Sudan. It was made up of the four main rebel tribes that refused to sign the May 2006 peace agreement. As a result, both the Sudanese government and the Janjaweed militia launched a large offensive against the National Redemption Front and the Darfurian people, resulting in more deaths and more displacements. This recent fighting, which took place along the Chad border, has left nearly a quarter of a million refugees cut off from aid. Our UNICEF agency recently reported that around 80 infants die each day in Darfur as a result of malnutrition."

We listened to the tales of woe described by the secretary and nodded our heads in commiseration.

The secretary continued: "One of the UN's departments is the department of "safety and security" **(DSS)** which contains a division of "field support service." This division maintains a very secret organization that gathers the intelligence required to follow terrorist organizations. My Under-Secretary in charge of the department, David Monet, devised an apparently workable plan intended to plant the SOMA inhalers within both the Janjaweed militiamen and the rebels, and to test their possible peace-inducing property. David, can please, describe your plan?"

David Monet said: "For fooling the Janjaweed I have an Iranian operative who possesses forged papers as an authorized arms dealer. He will purchase AK-47's (Kalashnikov) assault rifles, millions of rounds of ammunition and RPG rocket propelled grenades from an arms factory in Poland. He will offer these arms to the Janjaweed ostensibly as a gift from the Islamic Revolutionary Guard of Iran to Sudan, in order to "further the Arab-Islamic cause". The arms will be transported to the Port of Sudan in the Red Sea by a chartered boat and transferred into the hands of the Janjaweed militiamen. Our operative will instruct the Janjaweed leaders to keep the whole operation secret even from the Pro-Janjaweed Sudanese or Iranian government officials, saying that since it is so covert, they will refuse to admit any knowledge of it . . .

Our operative will also offer SOMA to the Janjaweed, in the guise of alleged Benzedrine inhalers. The Janjaweed leaders will gladly accept them since it is widely known that Benzedrine has euphoric and stimulating effects and is used by combatants for temporarily postponing their need for sleep when the desire for sleep may affect the success of a mission. The Benzedrine can also allow combatants to keep fighting for scores of hours. The SOMA inhalers will carry fake labels in Iranian and Arabic that will say that they were manufactured by an Iranian pharmaceutical company and will direct the militiamen how to use them. Since the SOMA inhalers will, hopefully, induce euphoria and serenity, the Janjaweed militiamen will happily continue to use them as if it they were the Hashish that they generally smoke, and will hopefully, become peaceful! We need not worry about the supplied arms, since the now peace-loving Janjaweed will stop using them . . . If the SOMA will not work, the damage will not be that great, since the Janjaweed militiamen are already armed to their teeth.

David Monet then added: "I will repeat the same type of scam with the National Redemption Front leaders. I will use the services of another agent of mine who is a high-ranking official within the Ministry of Defense of the Chad government. He will approach his boss and will say that he got in touch with a polish armament factory and managed to obtain a very cheap deal for arms (such as those supplied to the Janjaweed . . .) and many thousands of "Polish" Benzedrine inhalers. He will tell the Minister of Defense of Chad that if the deal he will authorize the deal, it will be an excellent chance to support the National Redemption Front in their fight against the well-armed Arab Janjaweed militias. He will, ostensibly, buy the arms for the Chad Republic at a low cost, but will secretly add the rest of the money to the Polish company from UN funds. If the Janjaweed militia and the National Redemption Front will proclaim their wish to cease fighting, the conclusion is obvious – the SOMA worked.

All UN officials in the meeting, including our team and "our" billionaires, applauded David Monet for his marvelous idea and he bowed in great satisfaction.

27

Year 2022

In the wake of Darfur's successful "clinical trial", Ravi Meenakshee convened the UN General Assembly to a special emergency session. Prior to the session which, according to the secretary, was going to astound the whole world, the press Secretary of the United Nations asked for and received coverage from most of the major Tri-D stations in the world. The secretary allowed two days for preparation, advertising and public relations. During these two days, newspaper and Tri-D correspondents all over the world speculated about the possible reason for the special emergency session: "aliens from outer space contacted the UN, considering it to be the governing authority of all earth ("take me to your leader!"), or that scientists have discovered an ultimate drug for all types of cancer, or god forbid, a very lethal virus was discovered in some remote corner in the world and is extremely contagious and incurable" and so on . . . . Bookies all over

211

the world started bets on the correct reason for the special emergency session.

Finally, the time for the session came, and the UN secretary stood on the speaker's podium and said: "Citizens of the world! It is with great happiness and feelings of awe that I am going to describe a wonderful unparalleled invention made by four scientists from the Department of Neurochemistry, Harvard University School of Medicine—Professor John Novick, Dr. Benjamin Fond, Miss Deborah Cohen and Mrs. Lucia Fernandez. These scientists have invented a marvelous drug called SOMA, which is going to revolutionize the whole world! The SOMA is a non-addictive happiness—and serenity-inducing drug that can also cure all human mental disorders and all forms of depression! This drug is going to bring real "peace in our time" to the whole world—not like the "peace" achieved in 1938 by Neville Chamberlain, Great Britain's prime minister, by allowing Hitler to conquer Poland . . . We are sponsoring this wonderful drug and will distribute it throughout the whole world.

Very recently, many people the world have been utterly amazed by a very happy political event in Sudan: after long and terrible civil wars, all the fighting parties in Darfur and the Sudanese government have finally signed a comprehensive peace treaty. This tremendous achievement was secretly instigated by us! We gave the SOMA by subterfuge to all the fighting parties in Darfur and it transformed all combatants into euphoric, serene and peace-loving people! Based on this tremendous success, we are going to distribute the SOMA to the whole world, thus achieving the great aim of the UN to bring peace.

Billions of doses of this drug have already been secretly manufactured by the non-profit "climate" consortium of Bill Kelly and Warren Brooks that ostensibly pretended to try to reduce all greenhouse gases in the atmosphere!" The secretary stopped his address for a few seconds to let his words sink in, but could not continue: all the ambassadors to the UN and the heads of all governments that attended the plenary session rose up as one man and applauded. The secretary then called me, my team and Bill and Warren to the podium to share the accolades. The secretary continued: "Dear citizens of the world, the SOMA will be distributed, free of charge, to everybody through our World Food Program (WFP). Many additional centers will be established soon, in order to distribute the SOMA all over the world."

At the start, not all citizens of the world agreed to try the SOMA. The more cautious and paranoid ones among them waited to see what will happen. But soon all flocked to the many WFP distribution centers in each country to receive it. With time, the WFP was re-directed to distributing food and the UN established "UNSA" – the United Nations SOMA Agency—to distribute the SOMA.

As the sole distributor, The UN now wielded enormous power over the whole world and boycotted several countries: those that supported terrorist activities, produced weapons of mass destruction and that were ruled by corrupt dictators who exploited and abused their people. The ban on these black-list countries yielded immediate and impressive results: their citizens rebelled and ousted their belligerent corrupt governments and dictators in order to join the happy and peaceful family of all the world's nations. At long last, all the countries that had possessed nuclear weapons, dangerous warfare germs and toxic gases quickly destroyed them! In 2013 there were about 250 disputes and war sites in the world, and in 2014 the number dwindled to zero. This happy outcome led to a motion by all governments and countries in the world to create an UN-administered world government and thus, out of many nations, came one world government whose moto was "E pluribus unum – out of many (nations) one (world government)!"

28

Year 2022

"Dear viewers, as you know, Dr. Fond and I received Nobel prizes in 2014. I received the Prize for Medicine or Physiology in the concert hall of Stockholm, Sweden, from King Karl Gustav the 16th also for Professor Fond; while Dr. Fond received the peace prize, also on my behalf, from king Harald the 5th at the municipality house in Oslo, Norway. Let me describe to you "my" Nobel prize awarding ceremony in Stockholm: on each day during the Nobel week, one of the prize winners of that year gave a public address – the "Nobel lecture"—describing the work which earned him, or her, the prize. Finally, the day of the presentation of the prizes came. The presentation ceremony was conducted in the presence of the king, his family, honored guests, the members of the various Nobel Prize committees and relatives of the winners (including my wife Dr. Debra Cohen, my parents and my sister. Ben's family accompanied him to Oslo. Many Nobel laureates from past years also attended. Presentation speeches were given by various Swedish scientists – experts in field of each prize—praising the laureates and their discovery. Following that, His Majesty the King of Sweden handed each winner a diploma and a medal. The Ceremony was followed by a banquet at the Stockholm City Hall for about 1,300 people where the winners, one representative from each category, delivered their acceptance speech (also termed "banquet speech"). The reason that I am describing this ceremony to you is not to brag about it, but to present my somewhat perplexing acceptance speech and give you some food for thought . . . I spoke first, and this is what I said:

"Your Majesty, Your Royal Highness, Mr. President of the royal Swedish academy, Excellencies, Ladies and Gentlemen: Many Nobel laureates made inspiring and exciting speeches in this magnificent hall and, therefore, I will have to try my utmost to measure up to their high standards. I am a Science Fiction and Fantasy fan, and therefore I want to tell you a story that could, perhaps, shed light on how the idea of the development of the SOMA may have evolved in my mind. Is my story real, or is it just a dream that I had? I myself, do not know . . . Since we constantly enjoy the benefits of the SOMA, why should we really care how it came into being? Still, here it is:

About 79 earth-time years ago, a committee convened in one of the planets of our galaxy. This committee, whose formal name was "The galactic committee for the preservation of young sentient races", was made of several members of highly developed races that we call "extraterrestrial aliens" in Science-Fiction novels. The job of this committee was to locate sentient races in the galaxy that reached the ability to perform nuclear fission but as yet had not reached enlightenment and world peace, and to prevent them from blowing up their planets. The committee was convened in the wake of detection of nuclear explosions in New-Mexico and Japan. This committee, whose experience was immense in this kind of task, exercised various covert means to achieve their objective—they snatched humans into their spaceship, studied their anatomy, physiology and brain. These human guinea pigs were eventually returned befuddled to earth after a day or two with vague memories of aliens studying them. No wonder that there have been increasing reports in the last decades of alien UFOs in our atmosphere and of people claiming that they have been snatched by aliens . . . The committee studied the various neurotransmitters in the human brain and came to the conclusion that the administration of Endorphin to humans will turn them into moral and serene beings and will eliminate all feelings of greed, belligerency and depression. They have already used similar techniques successfully on other young sentient races in the galaxy that had different chemistries, but had responded favorably to the administration of suitable neurotransmitters.

Consequently, the members of the committee searched around for a neurochemist that was living alone, as I was at that time, and that could advance the development of a peace-inducing drug. As a result, the aliens drugged me, snatched me up to their spaceship and instilled the idea of the SOMA in my brain. This may be why before the actual start of our SOMA research I had from time to time, recurring strange dreams of aliens speaking to telepathically. Then one morning I woke up with the whole SOMA project mapped out in my brain. On coming to my office in the morning, I immediately started to draft a grant proposal to the National institute of mental health for the development of an Endorphin—based anti-depressant. I ought to mention that, luckily for the world, I was the best suitable candidate for such research since even before the aliens' intervention I had studied Endorphin and its effects quite extensively in my lab.

"Your Majesty, Your Royal Highness, Mr. President, Excellencies, Ladies and Gentlemen. This is my story. Accept or reject it if you wish. In fact, I am not even sure, myself, if it is real or just a hallucination or a dream that I have experienced." The audience sat fascinated and did not know whether to accept my story at face value, or just as a beautiful fairy tale or jest.

Then I added: "whether or not my story is true, I want to sing hosannas to the SOMA:

It made us serene, euphoric, loving and happy;

It cured all Humanity's mental diseases;

It strengthened our immune system and improved our general health;

It eradicated all crime from the world;

It stopped all wars, terrorist activities and conflicts between nations;

It eradicated all greed, racism and hunger and made us all charitable to one another;

It united us under a single world government and eliminated all chauvinism and narrow nationalism.

Finally, I would like to address the Nobel peace prize committee in Oslo: I have read the regulations of the nominating Nobel Prize committees and learned that each Nobel Prize laureate has the privilege of nominating candidates for next year's Nobel prizes. Although Bill Kelly and Warren Brooks had already won many acclaims, medals and accolades all over the world, in my opinion it is still not enough Therefore, I would like to nominate them as candidates for next year's Nobel peace prize. Without them the SOMA might not have come into being."

John completed his tri-D address and said: "Dear viewers, this is the end of my address. I would like to bid all of you a happy SOMA day or SOMA night, as the case may be in your time zones. Have a happy life and prosper and may God bless you all!"

Thus the epic broadcast came to its end. The newscaster thanked all the translators and the WBR-Tri-D's personnel, and his face faded out from the 3D Holovision "cube."

Epilogue

Dear readers,

You probably wonder whether the research outline that I drew in the book is only fictional or is scientifically sound. The answer is that this research plan is, indeed, feasible. Beta Endorphin is a neurotransmitter that alleviates pain and induces euphoria and the methods that I "invented" for its production and administration are scientifically possible. However, even if the Beta Endorphin would actually work in humans, its action can be only short-lived. Endorphin's receptors (which are also common to other Opioid drugs) are bound to develop tolerance within a short time, just as they do with Alcohol and Heroin, and to fail to induce pleasure and serenity.

Research activities intended to develop an ideal anti-depressant continue. For example, there is now a growing recognition that there exists a "happiness gene" that operates in those fortunate, enviable people who always seem to be cheerful! Genetic studies have proved that happiness and psychological stability are linked to the existence of two copies (one from both parents) of a gene called 5-HTTLPR, which was found to be responsible for the transport of Serotonin in the brain. Possibly, there could be more "happiness" genes.

All that remains for us to do is to hope that Pharmacology, or the developing science of Gene Therapy will allow us, still in our life-time, to reach the state of mind that was advocated by Guru Meher Baba: "Don't worry, be happy!"